When Smirnoff turned, Freya was ready. Smirnoff executed another Sinanju move, this time using her arm in a rapid swing thrust, followed by a leg sweep. Freya blocked the arm and leapt over her leg. She tried to strike Smirnoff in the neck, but Smirnoff ducked and grabbed Freya's arm. Using Freya's momentum against her, Smirnoff hurled her through the wall.

Freya twisted, but the impact of breaking through two-inch wall studs dazed her. She staggered to her feet, but her back hurt, making it hard to breathe and hold her center. Smirnoff followed through the hole and attacked.

Freya was afraid.

LEGACY

BOOK VII: 100 PROOF

Warren Murphy & Gerald Welch

LEGACY, Book VII: 100 Proof

By Warren Murphy and Gerald Welch

ISBN-13: 978-1-944073-51-0 (Destroyer Books)
ISBN-10: 1-944073-51-5

Requests for reproduction or interviews should be directed to: destroyerbooks@gmail.com

Official website: www.facebook.com/LegacyBookSeries

Cover and other artwork by Gerald Welch

Published by Destroyer Books/Warren Murphy Media
Edited by Devin Murphy

First public printing: August 2018

A WORD FROM CHIUN, MASTER OF SINANJU EMERITUS

Discerning reader, if you seek truth and enlightenment, I beseech you to put this book down with all haste. You will not find it here. Despite my generous offering to the unfocused scribbler who swore an oath that he would share the truth and glory of Sinanju, he has proven to be nothing more than another feeble-minded scribe. He has not even written my words in Korean! I should be dismayed, but my experience is that all scribblers are inveterate liars and reprobates, and this one is no exception.

What should be a noble and inspiring passage of cultural and historical importance has instead been diluted into what even other foolish whites call 'pulp fiction.'

Thus, you are denied the true exploits of how I, Chiun, the most venerated and exalted Master of Sinanju, out of my infinite grace, bestowed the gift of a momentous death journey upon one who has been a minor help to Sinanju on occasion. You shall not witness poetry commemorating the event in these pages, nor shall you be provided accurate mind pictures of my beloved home of Sinanju.

Instead, you hold in your hands pages and pages of a wandering absurdity that attempts to turn my luggage carter into a hero. I only allowed this story to see print because the mongrel in question reminds me in many distressing ways of my son, Remo.

If you truly seek adventure, honor and courage, you will have to seek it elsewhere. And if you had the lamentable misfortune of exchanging gold for this volume, then I, knowing whites as I do, can say nothing more than you should have known better.

With moderate tolerance for you all, I remain

Chiun

Master of Sinanju.

To Mason:

May you remain ever curious

Gerald Welch

PROLOGUE

THREE DECADES AGO

Dr. Vanessa Carlton knew she would have to die. She had been born with a "once in a lifetime brain," an intellect so vast it outpaced Albert Einstein and Leonardo Da Vinci. So great was her 'Alpha Class' mind that when she graduated from Cornell at fifteen, the United States military invoked a rarely-used law to declare her mind a weapon of mass destruction. She became a ward of the state, and NASA her legal guardian.

At first, Vanessa though the special treatment was funny. Soon, however, her work became classified at such a high level that even her own boss was not allowed to know what she was doing. She laughed when she found out that they had even classified what she chose to eat, but her amusement stopped when was told she was not allowed to walk in public any more, unless she was escorted by a team of armed guards. Eventually, only a handful of top-level NASA personnel were even allowed to know of her existence. Her life of the mind had become a life of utter solitude.

When she turned 20, Vanessa was moved to the Wilkins Laboratory, a three-story secure facility designed specifically for her. While her handlers believed that they had provided everything that Vanessa could want or need, she looked at the dull gray walls and saw a prison.

Things got better a few years later, when they brought another genius to the Wilkins Laboratory, a young boy named Taylor, whose upbringing in poor, rural Georgia did nothing to dim the fires of his immense intellect. Despite their age difference, Vanessa welcomed Taylor's company. Together, they developed groundbreaking new technology for NASA, but when they worked together to disable building's security system, using nothing more than a thermostat and a light socket, NASA had to separate them.

Though Taylor had been half her age, she had found someone who was able to fully communicate with her. After he left, knew that she had to do something to fix her loneliness. She began drinking heavily, but during her sober hours, her thoughts turned to friends — and her lack of them. Some of Taylor's notes on robotics were promising, so Vanessa began using them as blueprints to design her own friends.

Like every other problem she had encountered in her life, Vanessa broke the problem down into individual components. Analyzing what she was missing in life, she decided that there were three types of people that one favorably interacts with: family, friends, and lovers. Since she obviously could not be related to an android, that left friends and lovers. She started by designing 'personality software,' using it to build a self-aware cart. It was smart enough to recognize voice commands, and its sensors were good enough that it could travel from anywhere in the laboratory to any other. It could even bring her food and drinks on command.

As she continued working on her androids, she spent long hours confiding into the flat metal cart, who could only offer sympathy for not understanding the complexity of human emotion. To Vanessa, it was still just a thing. It needed to be humanized. It needed a name. Looking at the empty bottle in her hand, she looked at the cart and named it Mr. Seagrams.

On her next security-accompanied "field trip," Vanessa went to a department store, and was fascinated by a new line of hyper-realistic mannequins. Unlike the blank white armless and headless mannequins she had seen before, these actually looked like women, complete with eye makeup and lipstick. She requested some to be sent to her lab. Her requests, as odd as they had become over the years, were never questioned, so the next day she had four mannequins; three male and one female.

She quickly found out that the plastic mannequins were very fragile, so she returned again to Taylor's notes, in which he had sketched out a self-replicating corporeal virus. It had been designed so that once an object was set into a specific shape, the virus would maintain the shape's consistency. If a piece was ever damaged or lost, the virus would convert surrounding material to return the part to its original shape. Over the next few months, she continued refining and improving on Taylor's formula, making it more efficient and resilient. Even though the medical and military applications of self-repairing material would have been vast, to share it with her supervisors would have interrupted her quest to build android friends, so Vanessa kept her research and her work secret, known to no one but herself.

She eventually created three males, Mr. Gordons, Mr. Daniels, and Mr. Smirnoff — friend, warrior and lover. Eventually, she presented NASA with Mr. Gordons as an android smart enough to survive space travel. Her supervisors were thrilled.

Though he still needed serious work, Daniels was an adequate demonstration of a direct military application.

The code for Smirnoff, however, was more advanced than the other two and far more personal. As such, it took more time, so she used the same code for both the male and female Smirnoff mannequins.

Vanessa found that she was spending more time on the female version of Smirnoff, augmenting her code. She even created a basic binary emotional response inside Smirnoff.

One morning, she noticed that Mr. Gordons was missing. He called her later to give her a status update on his survival and she told him to return to the lab, but he would not listen. He explained that if he was going to survive, he needed creativity, something she had only given the Smirnoff models. Unable to comprehend the limitations of his own code, Mr. Gordons hung up.

Vanessa began to worry. His programming was such that he would choose his own survival over any other available solution. Then she found out that Mr. Gordons had killed several people and almost crashed the entire U.S. economy.

That was when she knew that she was going to die. Gordons' crimes had become too large to ignore. So when a man with thick wrists named Remo and an elderly Korean man came along asking about Gordons, she knew why they were there. They claimed to be from some generic government organization, but she knew they had to be from some kind of top secret hit squad. The elderly Korean was so polite that Vanessa was almost embarrassed to die at his hand.

As Vanessa died, and all of her work was destroyed, Smirnoff remained safely ensconced in her charging station.

Though she was in stasis, she heard everything that happened. She was not programmed for survival like Mr. Gordons, or combat like Mr. Daniels, so even if she had been free of her pod, she could not have done anything to save her creator.

Vanessa had isolated Smirnoff's personality to the role of 'lover,' in contrast to the other androids' more forceful roles of 'warrior' and 'survivor.' Smirnoff copied their files and incorporated them into her own code. It took months to balance the personalities, but Smirnoff eventually became an amalgamation of all of Vanessa's creations. She was a lover, a warrior, and most importantly, Smirnoff was now a survivor.

Until she was could access new data networks, there was nothing left for Smirnoff to do or to learn. To conserve resources, she placed herself in hibernation, and knew that someday, she would avenge her creator.

CHAPTER ONE

Over four hundred NASA scientists were crammed into an old concrete building, the air condition system of which was fighting a losing battle. The building was one of NASA's original auditoriums, built in the late fifties to house scientists from around the world. The aisles were packed with scientists in stained white smocks, and the air was redolent with B.O. and Cheetos.

"How many NASA scientists can they fit inside one building?" Randy McCabe asked. The pudgy thirty-five-year old had a thin face and pasty skin, resembling a human bowling pin, but he was one of NASA's leading robotics experts. His lab partner, Roderick Zelensky, was a tall, thin man with small eyes and thick glasses. He peered over the crowd of scientists, trying to find his supervisor without any luck.

"That sounds like the setup to a bad joke," Zelensky replied in a thick Eastern European accent.

"I don't like this," McCabe said. "This guy thinks he can flip a switch and we're all suddenly going to change everything we've been working on for years."

Eddie Bruce, the source of the scientists' anxiety, stood at the front of the hall and rubbed his eyes in frustration. At fifty-three, he was too old to babysit a bunch of people smart enough to know better. Over the past fifteen minutes, he had tried to explain the situation to some of the smartest minds on Earth, but he could only make himself understood by speaking like he was addressing preschoolers — which is also how they responded.

"I can't make it any simpler than this: NASA is returning to its original mission," he said slowly.

One of the scientists stood to his feet. "That's…that's just…you're insane!" he stammered. "We've evolved past space exploration!"

"Do you think you're a rocket scientist?" another shouted from the back. "Because I am!"

"This is not a request," Eddie said. "This is a directive. NASA will be returning to space exploration. We're going to build a lunar colony and land on Mars within the next twenty years. Whether you will still be here depends entirely on you."

The collection of scientists groaned in unison.

"How dare you!" a scientist who looked barely old enough to shave screamed. "My studies on the theoretical mating habits of fruit flies have won *twelve* international awards!"

"Well, actually, that's an easy one," Eddie said with a smile. "Unless you can come up with something that is applicable to our new mission, sir, you will need to look for another job...perhaps internationally, and certainly not theoretically."

The scientist's jaw dropped open, but nothing came out.

"I want all of you to listen to me very carefully," Eddie said, leaning forward. "NASA doesn't need any dead weight."

The crowd of scientists became quiet. No one had ever spoken to them this way. Zelensky continued scanning the crowd for his supervisor, but there were so many scientists and most were crying so hard that it was difficult to identify anyone.

"We've been looking at your books over the past six months and, with a few rare exceptions, it seems that you've spent the past twenty years wasting taxpayers' money on unicorns and rainbows. That ends today."

A few scientists began silently weeping. This was almost worse than the election.

"Every project that does not involve an active exploratory mission will be reviewed on a case-by-case basis," Eddie said. "All non-critical funding will be halted until your departments can pass a basic feasibility review."

As the crowd erupted in outrage, McCabe could barely blink as he considered the full weight of the words.

"We're finished," he said.

Zelensky finally spotted his supervisor standing toward the front of the room and grabbed McCabe by the sleeve. In the chaos, no one saw them leave the lecture hall.

"Where are we going?" McCabe asked.

"Matthews is up front," Zelensky said. "He'll be stuck here for hours trying to calm everyone down."

"So?"

"If he's here, then he's not at his computer."

"Dude, if we get caught on his computer…"

"What will they do, fire us?" Zelensky asked with a grin.

"They'll throw us in jail!" McCabe whispered loudly. "Who would take care of Mr. Knuckles?"

"If you don't have a job, you won't have money to feed your turtle! Look, all I have to do is put a backdoor in and then we can…modify our records."

Zelensky padded their records to show compliance with the new directives. So, when their boss showed up four days later, they were not worried. James Matthews was a crusty old NASA bureaucrat who started with NASA in the late eighties. He had fallen behind the technological curve sometime during Windows XP and was no longer able to understand the specifics of his own department. Thus, his department did whatever they wanted. If he ever asked questions, they merely responded with tech noise, and he silently stroked his chin as if he understood.

McCabe and Zelensky were able to set their own work schedules, coming up with just enough nonsense to satisfy the old man's queries. The best part was that since the work was theoretical, there was no deadline or need to show actual progress.

"Hey Jim," McCabe greeted, smiling.

"It's time for your review," Matthews said. "You understand none of this is personal."

A nervous glance was exchanged between McCabe and Zelensky. This was not the boss they had prepared for. He seemed far sterner than usual.

"Uh, right," McCabe said, leading him into their office. "I'm sure that you've seen the important work we've been doing."

James stopped and turned to look McCabe in the eye. "I don't think you understand, Dr. McCabe. Your department was reviewed weeks ago. I'm only here to give you the results."

McCabe began coughing and grabbing for his heart.

Matthews coughed and wiped his nose on his sleeve.

"I'm sorry to say that senior officials looked at your proposed workload and declined it. All of it."

Zelensky's eyes went wide with shock. "But, sir…the military applications!"

Matthews skipped a few pages on his clipboard until he found a paragraph.

"'*The targeted broadcast of alpha waves has shown no potential for theoretical — much less practical — field usage and is therefore not in line with departmental directives.*'"

"They just don't understand!" McCabe erupted. "This will end all wars! If we see an area of contention, we just flood the area with alpha waves. The targets will calm down, eliminating the very need for weapons!"

Matthews smiled in empathy, even though he did not understand what he had heard.

"Continuing to the last page…ah, here. '*Recommend they generate real-world applications suitable for target mission of lunar colony or vacate offices in ninety days.*'"

"Ninety days? But we're…" McCabe could not finish his sentence before starting to sob.

Matthews produced a piece of paper and had both men sign at the bottom.

"Alright boys, today's my last day. You may not have noticed, but I'm starting to fall behind the curve. Been thinking about retirement, maybe buying a boat; this shake-up made it an easy decision. You guys better get your act together, because the new sheriff isn't going to look the other way."

"Thanks for nothing, Matthews," Zelensky said.

McCabe exploded the moment Matthews walked out the door.

"What can we do in ninety days?"

Zelensky stifled a smile. McCabe was panicking as planned.

"Wait a minute," he said, snapping his fingers as if each click would trigger a memory. "Maybe…oh, what was her name? The crazy smart scientist lady who worked for NASA a long time ago…had her own building."

"The old Wilkins Lab?" McCabe asked. "That thing's been shut down for years."

"What if I told you that we could work there…with new tech and no budget?" Zelensky asked dramatically, grabbing McCabe by the shoulders. "You told me that you came to NASA to change the world!"

"I don't know, man. That was a long time ago."

"Just give it ninety days," Zelensky said, holding his fist out. "Mr. Knuckles needs you to keep this job."

McCabe reluctantly smiled and returned the fist bump.

"Ninety days it is!" McCabe said. "For Mr. Knuckles!"

"For Mr. Knuckles!" Zelensky replied. "Go home. We'll meet at the Wilkins building first thing in the morning."

Zelensky watched McCabe leave. He knew McCabe well enough to know that he would go home, sing to his turtle and spend the rest of the night playing Planet Warmaker. Zelensky looked out the window, making sure that McCabe drove away in his Prius. When he knew he was alone, he sent a one-word text message to an encrypted number. His cell phone rang within the minute.

"Progress report," a crisp baritone demanded. The man's accent was European, but not as pronounced as Zelensky's. Precision was chiseled into each vowel.

"I messed up our records like you suggested," Zelensky said. "They had no choice but to shut us down."

"Excellent. Is McCabe onboard?"

"Yes, sir. We will begin tomorrow," Zelensky said. "What about my parents?"

"Just keep me informed," Helmut Belisis said, hanging up the phone.

Helmut subconsciously scratched his newly-shaved chin before taking a slow drink from his snifter of brandy. He had had a beard for so long that the skin of his lower face felt soft and alien to his touch. But he needed a change. Helmut was director of an organization named VIGIL that had just suffered the largest setback in its history. Worse, Helmut knew that the disaster was partially due to his own arrogance.

After most of VIGIL's leadership was killed in a single attack, Helmut struggled to identify any structural problems with the organization that had secretly and successfully influenced nations across the world for over a millennium.

VIGIL had been formed by an Iberian monk who had looked to the skies, not for God, but for knowledge. This man knew that it would only be a matter of time before disease and war overwhelmed the human race, and man would go extinct. He began to form a community that would secretly use their influence to ensure mankind's survival for the next thousand years.

Over time, this organization accumulated wealth and power, hiding behind such publicly-known organizations as the Knights Templar and the Freemasons. Its membership fostered thinkers like Botticelli, Raphael, Vasari, and Salieri. Their mission all boiled down to population control: the greater the population, the larger the number that would survive a cataclysm or war.

The full resources of VIGIL were allocated to bringing World War II to a close, which was the first time that VIGIL stepped out of the shadows and began actively manipulating world governments. Their agents infiltrated the governments of every major nation on Earth. But in doing so, they sacrificed secrecy for power, and in doing so, VIGIL weakened itself with exposure.

It did not take long for Helmut to realize that VIGIL had simply outgrown its original design. The solution was also easy, though difficult to contemplate: VIGIL would have to go back to working in the shadows. The international prestige, fancy yachts and country clubs would be abandoned as a warning to future Directors about the danger of hubris. Helmut took a moment to savor his scotch before punching the intercom button.

"Sir?" his assistant answered.

"Redford, assemble a strike team," he said. "Tell them to meet me in D.C."

CHAPTER TWO

His name was Stone and he glided softly across the deep orange sands of the Arizona desert. His movements kept pace with the cool morning breeze that chilled the morning ground. He tried to move as quietly as he could into the shack behind Sunny Joe's house, but the door hinges squeaked to life as he entered. He tiptoed to the center of the small building and pulled the light chain, revealing a thin man sitting on a large stone at the front. Tuffs of long gray hair spilled out of the back of his grandfather's cowboy hat.

"How did I do?" Stone asked, obviously pleased with himself.

"I guess if you drove the truck up, it could have been louder," Sunny Joe said.

"C'mon, except for the door, no one but you would have heard anything," Stone protested. "I thought it was okay."

Sunny Joe cocked his head in disbelief.

"When did 'okay' become acceptable with you? Is that something the SEALs taught you? I sure didn't."

"I was pretty quiet," Stone said.

"You were only quiet because you gave it your full attention. Nicotine is running your system ragged, son. You can't control your body, and Sinanju depends on self-control."

"I'm going to start calling you Camel Joe if you don't lay off the cigarette sermons," Stone said and then took a deep breath. He felt the little tickle of nicotine as it wormed through his system. "Sorry, Grandpa. Look, I want to quit, I really do."

Sunny Joe stepped down until he stood eye-to-eye with Stone.

"You're not progressing, son. In fact, you're losing ground."

"Is that's why Freya's not here? This is some kind of remedial Sinanju?"

"You said it, I didn't," Sunny Joe said, placing his hand on Stone's shoulder. "Sinanju ain't for everyone."

"I know."

"Then why are you here?" Sunny Joe asked. "Do you even know?"

"No," Stone admitted after a pause. "At first, I thought I'd just learn a few things from you and go back to being a merc, but the more I learn, the more I know that I need to learn."

"Don't think I haven't seen you trying to insert your SEAL training for Sinanju moves. It'll get you killed, son."

"I'm trying to be a 'best of both worlds' warrior."

"There's no such thing."

"How do you know, Grandpa? Has anyone even tried?"

"Okay, fine. Let's work in your SEAL world," Sunny Joe said. He motioned to several panes of glass sitting against the wall. "We'll start with something basic."

"What's all the glass for?" Stone asked.

"A simple test. Tell me; how would a SEAL punch a hole in that window?"

Stone smiled. Sunny Joe was actually listening.

"I'd strike it with my elbow, aiming slightly below the center, minimizing personal damage and sound, while maximizing damage to the glass."

"Show me," Sunny Joe said.

Stone always knew when Sunny Joe had a 'greater truth' to show him. It usually started with something simple, and ended up with something he thought was impossible. Stone had no idea how he could tie it into breaking glass, so he pulled his arm back and concentrated. He would show Sunny Joe what the best of both worlds actually looked like. He would use his SEAL training to determine the course of action and then use his Sinanju training to follow through. Stone swung his arm, leading with his elbow and the window easily shattered. Shards of glass exploded on the rock, scattering across the dirt outside.

"No biggie," Stone said.

"Your SEAL training just got in the way of your mission."

"Really?" Stone asked. There was no way Sunny Joe could pull a lesson out of breaking a window. "How's that?"

"I said a hole. You destroyed the pane. And you had to pull your arm back to build up the necessary force."

"So what?" Stone almost shouted, holding up a victorious finger. "I wasn't a science nerd, but even I remember that mass times acceleration — *that's speed*, Grandpa — equals force."

"If you can't generate force, then yes, you have to build up speed. But it's the least efficient way to get the job done."

Stone almost smirked. He had heard some crazy things come out of his grandpa's mouth and though he had always somehow proved his point, there was no way he could win this one.

"Tell you what," Stone said with a smile. "You *prove* that speed isn't needed to 'generate the force' or whatever, and I'll do Freya's chores for a month."

"Are you just wanting to make your sister happy next month?"

"Har har," Stone said.

"See the window you just punched?"

Sunny Joe placed another pane of glass in front of Stone.

"What if I told you to punch the smallest hole you could with your finger?"

Stone glanced at the window and then back at Sunny Joe. "What's the catch?"

"No catch. Punch a hole in the glass with your finger. As small as you can."

Stone looked at the window and took a deep breath to center himself. He smiled at Sunny Joe and then punched his finger through the window, leaving a hole large enough for his fist to pass through.

"That wasn't hard."

"You splintered the glass," Sunny Joe said. "And the hole is far too large."

"That's what happens when you punch your finger through glass."

"Not if you do it right."

Stone crossed his arms. He looked at the hole in the window and then back at Sunny Joe.

"I know you're trying to tell me something, but I don't get it."

"Punch a hole just large enough for your finger."

"That's impossi…" Stone began, but knew that any time he said that, he always had to eat his own words. "Okay, show me."

Sunny Joe placed a smaller pane on the stone and with blinding speed, punched his finger through the window. Stone was barely able to see the finger as it appeared to pass through the window. He did not hear the glass break. There was a small *psssht* sound and Sunny Joe's finger exited the other side. When he pulled his finger back, a small hole appeared where his finger had been.

"Wow," Stone said, impressed. "Sorry, Grandpa, but while I'm sure that took extreme control, it's still mass times acceleration."

"Really? You try."

Stone concentrated. He knew that Sunny Joe's finger had to be traveling insanely fast and with extreme control so that it didn't move up or down even a micron. Without pulling his finger back, Stone thrust his hand forward and his finger went through the glass. It cracked the entire pane but produced a jagged hole slightly larger than his finger.

"There!" Stone bragged. "Mass times acceleration!"

Sunny Joe smiled. "There are cracks."

"But I'll *get* better and eventually, there won't be any cracks."

"There will always be cracks the way you do it."

Stone looked closely at the hole Sunny Joe made and stuck his finger inside. The edges of the hole were actually smooth on the inside, as it if had been polished.

"Your finger has weight to it, so if you strike it fast enough and straight enough, you make a small hole."

"What if it wasn't moving fast at all?"

"You'd shatter the whole pane."

"You sure about that?" Sunny Joe asked.

Stone noticed the glint in his eye and instantly became cautious.

"Wait a minute, you're telling me that if you strike the glass slow, and I mean *really* slow, that you can still make a hole without any cracks?"

"Yup."

"*Three* months of Freya's chores says that you can't."

"You're gonna be the one to tell Freya," Sunny Joe said. "And I'll do you one better. I won't strike the glass at all."

Sunny Joe rested his index finger on the glass pane and smiled. Stone watched carefully as the slightest flutter of Sunny Joe's flexor tendons signaled a move. His finger passed through the glass as if it were melted plastic. There was barely a hum as his finger continued through until his knuckle rested against the front of the pane. When he pulled his finger out, Stone saw that the same smooth hole resulted.

"There is mass, and to move, there *is* acceleration," Sunny Joe explained. "But you don't have to multiply them to get results if you know what you're doing."

Stone's jaw dropped open and he lowered his face to the glass. It was just as smooth as the first hole Sunny Joe made.

"Holy crap," he said. "You did it to me again."

"You did it to yourself," Sunny Joe explained. "The more you cling to your SEAL training, and the longer you continue to smoke, the less you're gonna learn."

The hut door burst open, startling Stone. He turned to see Freya standing in the doorway. She looked like she was in shock.

"Grandfather!" she cried.

Sunny Joe had detected her swift approach and noticed that she had not bothered to cover the sound of her footsteps. He was going to reproach her for her sloppy entrance but heard the concern in her voice.

"It's Mick," she said. "Kathleen just took him to the hospital!"

CHAPTER THREE

The Wilkins Laboratory rose from a flat grassy plain, far away from the bustle of NASA's Washington, D.C. officers.

McCabe and Zelensky met in front of the building at eight.

"I don't know about this," McCabe said. "It's kinda spooky."

"That doesn't sound scientific or optimistic," Zelensky replied, producing a key.

"How'd you get that?"

"Relax, we're safe," Zelensky said, opening the door and turning on the lights.

The inside was a stark contrast to the outside. While the brick on the outside of the building had grown green from mildew, the inside was a pristine display of smooth lines and polished marble. Based on what he had heard about the place, McCabe had half-expected to see garbage cluttering the floor. It even smelled as though it had been cleaned the day before.

"I thought they said this place was trashed," McCabe said. "How are the lights still working?"

Zelensky grabbed his arm and pulled him to the side.

"You aren't gonna believe this, but I've been working on something."

"When?" McCabe asked.

McCabe thought that when Zelensky was not at the lab, he was playing video games. "I didn't want to show you until everything was ready. Let's go upstairs."

McCabe exited the elevator to the third floor. Zelensky smiled and motioned for him to follow. Every single room on the third floor was filled with millions of dollars of equipment.

"You mean to tell me that our department couldn't afford a new coffee machine, and you've had access to this?"

"There's a coffee machine in every room," Zelensky boasted. "I've been working here off and on for the past few weeks."

A small metal cart wheeled up to Zelensky by itself.

"What is thy bidding, my Master?" a thin voice asked.

McCabe jumped back.

"What is that?" he asked. It looked like a normal cart with a thick chrome brick mounted under the top.

"I am Mr. Seagrams," the cart replied.

"It's a waiter dummy, linked to the kitchen," Zelensky noted. "Try it. Ask for something."

"Okay, I want a large glass of milk," McCabe said.

"We are out of stock," Seagrams said.

"Well, I have to go to the store," Zelensky admitted. "Get us some chips, Seagrams."

The little cart obediently turned around and moved toward the kitchen.

"That's amazing!" McCabe said. "And you just found it here?"

"Oh, that's nothing! I found something a lot cooler than Seagrams. I didn't want to turn it on and risk damaging it, so I waited for you."

Zelensky led McCabe to the back end of what looked like a long closet. There was barely enough room for them to walk in. Zelensky pulled something at the end of the wall and the closet panels opened, exposing four pods. Three of the pods were empty, but the last was occupied by a female mannequin.

"What do you think?" Zelensky asked.

McCabe stood in front of the mannequin. Large cables led into the sides of its head and around its back.

"What is it?"

"The answer to our prayers!" Zelensky shouted. "NASA wants us to come up with something for exploration. Here it is!"

"I don't get it."

"We have three months. So, we just have to get this to work and we can say that this is the first phase of unmanned missions to the moon or whatever."

"I don't know, man. This has got to be some really old tech," McCabe grunted. "My flip phone is probably more advanced."

"All we have to do is get it working. The hardware's still in great shape. I'm just having some problems with the code."

"Ah, so that's why you need me."

"I'm telling you, this baby is our ticket. The terminal's over there."

Zelensky pointed to a small monitor displaying amber characters on a black screen. As the ancient code ran down the screen like a digital waterfall, McCabe became excited. Zelensky was right. He had first come to NASA to build robots that could terraform Mars for an eventual Earth colony. But those nerds in the Jet Propulsion Lab always one-upped him with their stupid rovers.

McCabe sat in front of the terminal and pressed the ENTER key. A solitary amber line began blinking, waiting for a command. McCabe's fingers flew across the keyboard, searching directories for a command structure.

"Weird…there's only one command. It's called "Breathe.exe"," he said.

"I already tried it," Zelensky said. "Nothing happens."

Seagrams wheeled back into the room with eight different bags of chips.

"Your chips, sire," it said.

Zelensky rolled his eyes.

"Sometimes you need to be a bit specific with this one," he said. "Thank you, Seagrams."

"It is my pleasure, sire."

McCabe ignored Zelensky's offer of chips. He was confused. Though the technology was clearly over a decade old, it was more modern than what he had been working on at their old office.

"This makes no sense," he said.

Zelensky shrugged his shoulders.

"That's what I was having a problem with. It won't accept any normal commands."

"It looks old, but this is a state-of-the-art custom operating system," McCabe said. "In fact, it's better than anything I've ever seen."

"Then why doesn't it work?" Zelensky asked.

"I don't know. I'll take a look at it."

"How long will that take?" Zelensky asked, exasperated.

"I'll let you know after a pizza. Extra pineapple."

As Zelensky left for the pizza joint down the block, he sent a text. The phone rang within seconds.

"McCabe's working on the software," Zelensky said. "In fact, he's pretty excited about it."

"How long do you anticipate it will take?" Helmut asked.

"He's really good with operating systems. Maybe a couple of days?"

"Have you read the report I sent?"

"Of course," Zelensky lied. He had only read the first few pages, which was more technobabble than even he liked.

"It cannot be emphasized strongly enough: when the unit awakens, it will establish a bond with its creator. Under no circumstances are you to allow the android to bond with either of you."

"Sir, please, I'll do whatever you want, but I need to know that my parents are safe."

"As long as you follow orders, they have nothing to worry about."

"Thank you, sir. I'm sorry about…"

"When the android wakes, you will say that Helmut Belisis is its creator and *immediately* contact me. I will take over from that point."

The phone hung up from the other side.

Twenty minutes later, Zelensky returned with the pizzas, but McCabe looked angry.

"Why didn't you tell me about Mr. Gordons?" he shouted.

Zelensky set the pizzas on the table. "How did you…?"

"I found your report. It said other androids were built, and the one they called Mr. Gordons actually killed people! You took me away from my Alpha Waves for *this*?"

Zelensky was embarrassed. Helmut had given him the notes with the strict understanding that no one else was allowed to see them.

"Calm down!" Zelensky commanded. "I had to make a decision. We could either do this, or be shut down!"

"How do we know this thing won't come to life and kill us in our sleep?"

Zelensky smiled. "Well, you obviously didn't read the report, or you'd know that each of the androids was built for a specific task. This one's a lover. If she wakes you up in the middle of the night, you're going to have a different problem."

McCabe's face flushed red.

"Oh."

"Look, let's just get this done so we can get funding for next year. Look, we'll even find a way to incorporate Alpha Waves."

McCabe stared hard at Zelensky before backing down.

"I'm not happy," he said. "But I'll do it."

Hours passed and Zelensky ended up falling asleep on a couch. McCabe did not notice. He was absorbed in computer code.

"That should have worked," he said, rubbing his eyes. "Hey man, I'm going to call it..." McCabe was interrupted by a sudden movement behind him.

The cables unplugged themselves from the android. McCabe heard soft whirring sounds as it stepped from its cocoon. The android looked around the lab, finally focusing on McCabe.

"Creator identification," it said. The voice was feminine, but with a metallic edge. McCabe cautiously walked toward it.

"I'm, uh, I'm Randy McCabe. I work here."

Smirnoff focused her eyes on him and McCabe felt as if he was being sized up.

"Creator identity established," Smirnoff said. "Creator Randy McCabe, I am Smirnoff."

"Smirnoff...like the drink?" McCabe asked.

"I am Smirnoff, like the drink," Smirnoff corrected.

"No...you can just call yourself Smirnoff if you want," McCabe said.

"I am Smirnoff. All systems are operating within tolerances, Creator Randy McCabe."

Zelensky was slow to awaken, but on hearing the android say 'Creator Randy McCabe,' his eyes shot open and he stumbled from the couch.

"No! No! Wait!" he screamed, running toward the android.

Smirnoff turned toward Zelensky, placing herself between him and McCabe in a defensive posture. For a moment, Zelensky forgot all about Helmut's threats against his family as Smirnoff walked toward him. Her movements were precise, silent, and chilling.

"Identify yourself," she said.

"I'm…co-creator Zelensky."

"There is only one creator," Smirnoff said. "His name is Creator Randy McCabe."

"Zelensky's my friend," McCabe said. "He's not a threat, seriously."

"Zelensky has been classified as not a threat," Smirnoff said, relaxing her stance.

Zelensky began to hyperventilate. He was going to have to make a phone call and explain that the android had bonded with McCabe. He said a quick prayer for his parents and headed downstairs to make the call.

CHAPTER FOUR

The Douglas hospital was a fifteen-minute drive from the reservation, but Sunny Joe made it in ten. He pulled into the emergency entrance and tossed his keys to Stone.

"Park it!" he shouted.

Sunny Joe dashed to the emergency room door and Freya raced after him. He approached the nurse at the front counter. Sunny Joe recognized the nurse.

"Gina, where's Mick?"

The nurse nodded to the door.

"Room three," Gina said. "Kathleen's already there."

Sunny Joe entered the room to see Mick attached to multiple machines. Kathleen stood at the back wall, fresh tears following the dried path of earlier tears down her face.

Sunny Joe motioned for Freya to stand back to allow the nurses space to finish their work. The last nurse to leave the room looked at Sunny Joe and sadly shook her head.

"Billy!" Kathleen cried from Mick's bed side. "They say he's not going to make it!"

Sunny Joe ignored Kathleen and leaned over Mick.

"Doctors only know what they're taught to know," Sunny Joe said, reaching around the wires to Mick's back. "It's not their fault they don't know how the body works."

Sunny Joe took a few seconds manipulating the nerves up and down his spine and Mick's body deflated.

"What did you just do?" Kathleen asked.

"Turned off his receptors. He was still in pain. Where's Doc Hodges?"

"I don't know," Kathleen said. "He told me that Mick isn't going to leave the hospital this time. Billy, whatever Sinanju magic you have, you better work it now."

Sunny Joe lowered his head.

"I've done all I can do."

Mick stirred, looking around, trying to focus his eyes on something; anything. When he saw Kathleen, he smiled. Kathleen grabbed his hand.

"You guys are awful loud," he whispered. "Can't a dead guy get any rest?"

Mick turned to look at Sunny Joe. There was a sense of acceptance in his eyes.

"Something's broke on the inside this time, Sunny Joe. I can feel it."

"I know," Sunny Joe admitted. "I'm trying to make you comfortable."

"Billy's doing everything he can," Kathleen said. "We're gonna get you home."

"We both know that ain't true," Mick said, attempting a smile. "These machines and Sunny Joe are the only reason I'm still breathing."

"It's time to make your peace," Sunny Joe said.

"Don't you *dare* talk to him like that!" Kathleen shouted. "He's still alive!"

Mick winced. "Hon, please…you gotta stop yelling."

Mick took a deep breath and glanced out the window as the morning sun illuminated the tree outside. He had seen the beautiful orange and pink hues scattered through his own window a thousand times, but he had never stopped to give it his full attention. Then he turned his gaze to Kathleen. The soft brown eyes he had fallen in love with locked with his and in that moment, she knew he was right.

"You need to call the kids," he said.

"Donna and Mariella have already booked flights," Kathleen said. "Leo is overseas, but I left a message."

"And Vic?"

Kathleen looked down.

"He said that he wants to wait at the house."

Silence filled the room.

"Anything I can do?" Sunny Joe asked.

"You can get me a new football," Mick said, attempting a laugh that erupted into a series of coughs.

Freya looked confused.

"I do not understand," she said.

"When we were about twelve, well, let's just say that I didn't display the level of control a Master of Sinanju is supposed to possess. One day, we're playing football. I got mad at Mick…"

"Over me," Kathleen added.

"Yep, over that one," Sunny Joe said, nodding to Kathleen. "Let's just say that after I kicked his football, there wasn't much left."

"I swore that I'd still be complaining about it on my deathbed," Mick said and the smiles slowly began to disappear. Mick looked at his lifelong friend and placed his hand on top of Sunny Joe's.

"Bill, I want to be buried in the Korean village."

"What?" Sunny Joe asked.

Mick stared at Freya.

"I've seen the bridge between the House and the Tribe," he said with tears in his eyes. "She's standing right there. But I know I won't live to cross it."

"Mick, I don't know what I can do," Sunny Joe said, but Mick began coughing and waving his hands.

"Let an old friend die thinking his last request will be taken care of."

Mike Hodges, the reservation doctor, entered the room. A middle-aged man with a full head of white hair, the wrinkles on his face indicated a lifetime of smiling, which made them seem warped as he frowned.

"Doc," Sunny Joe said.

"I hope Kathleen told you what's going on," he said. "I've gotta say, Sunny Joe, I don't know what else we can do at this point."

Sunny Joe lowered his head.

"Right now, the best thing we can do is give Mick some time to rest."

Sunny Joe stood but held Mick's hand. "Don't you worry. I'll find a way to get you home."

As Sunny Joe and Freya left, they saw Stone standing near the door in the waiting room.

"They wouldn't let me go in," Stone said. "How is he?"

"Not good," Sunny Joe said.

The walk to the truck was slow and the stillness in his grandfather told Stone all he needed to know. As Sunny Joe cranked his truck, he turned to Stone.

"I need to speak to your boss."

"Cole? Why?"

"I have to find a way to keep a promise I just made."

Stone pulled out his cell and dialed a number. The bouncy tones of an electronic supermarket began blaring and Stone pressed the number one over and over until the music stopped.

"Please leave a message," a mechanical voice said.

"I want to make a complaint," Stone said.

The line beeped twice and Stone handed the phone to Sunny Joe.

"He's not gonna be happy," Stone said. "He's a miser about phone time."

"I can handle it," Sunny Joe said as the line picked up on the other end.

"This is an unscheduled call," Ben said. "What is the situation?"

"This isn't Stone," Sunny Joe said. "Before you get upset, I told him to call."

"Good morning, Mr. Roam," Ben said. "Is there a problem with Stone and Freya's training?"

There was a momentary pause.

"I don't like asking for favors and I sure don't like owing them."

"What can I do for you?" Ben asked.

"I need to get a friend of mine to the village of Sinanju."

"Sinanju? As in the North Korean village?"

"He doesn't have much time."

"Have you been watching the news, Mr. Roam? It's not that simple."

"Then make it simple."

"Mr. Roam, we are all but at war with North Korea. There is no way I can get you anywhere near the village of Sinanju."

"There's got to be something you can do."

"I'm sorry, Mr. Roam. North Korea is too hot right now. Perhaps when this calms down I could pull some strings, but I'm sorry. Right now, there's nothing I can do."

Sunny Joe hung up the phone.

"What happened?" Stone asked.

"Your boss said no. But I've got a few strings of my own," Sunny Joe said, removing a scrap of paper from his wallet and dialing numbers.

CHAPTER FIVE

"The leg has got to come off," the doctor said, his eyebrows and shoulders pulled down by the weight of the world.

The young patient cast a worried glance to his girlfriend, who stood seductively by his bed. A solitary tear floated just below her eye, as though it had been placed there by an eye dropper. Her face displayed the abject pain of a broken heart.

"I understand, Doctor," the young man said.

The doctor left and his girlfriend leaned over the muscular teen, her tears cascading freely onto the hospital bed.

"Before they take away your leg…can we do it one more time, baby?"

The television screen did not crack as much as it imploded. The remote control had turned into a missile, piercing the screen with such precision that it dissolved into micro-shards and plastic dust.

A man from the next room instantly appeared in the doorway. He looked to be in his late thirties, wearing a dark shirt and chinos. He absently twisted his thick wrists as he assessed the situation.

"What the ding dong hell just happened?" Remo Williams asked.

"Your culture happened," Chiun, the Master of Sinanju Emeritus replied. "It has finally stolen the last splinter of joy that an old man might experience in this barbaric land."

Chiun glared at the television in front of him.

"Things like this did not happen before televisions became flat," he said.

"Little Father, the people who make TVs don't make the shows."

"So, you are claiming that this is just a coincidence?" Chiun asked suspiciously. "That this is all just the whimsical delirium of an old man?"

"I warned you not to watch that crap," Remo said, relaxing his stance. "Hollywood only has three gears these days: sex, violence and capes."

Chiun cocked his head and looked at Remo.

"What?" Remo asked.

"Did I ever tell you about Master Puk? He wore a cape."

"You've spent the better part of twenty years telling me how bad Puk was, but because he wore a cape, everything's copacetic? Little Father, I'm not going to wear a cape or a mask or the letter "R" on my chest."

"The mask would be an improvement," Chiun said.

The phone rang and time seemed to slow. Remo and Chiun made eye contact as an invisible gauntlet was thrown. Chiun raised his hand, motioning toward the phone while Remo dodged for it. A small hair pin tore through the air with the force of a missile. Remo grabbed the phone, twisting his body away from the pin at the last moment.

"Dammit, Chiun, I'm not going to keep buying phones every time you get pissed at a television show!"

"I should have spent more time training your appreciation of the arts. Or at least caring for the emotional well-being of your adoptive father. Woe is me, for in my advanced years, I have fallen into the reprobate hands of an ungrateful white."

Remo rolled his eyes and pulled the phone to his ear.

"Hello?"

The voice that spoke was one that Remo had not heard in nearly a year.

"Morning, son," Sunny Joe said.

The pause in the reply spoke for itself.

"What's wrong?" Remo asked.

"Stone and Freya are fine. I need to speak to the Chief," Sunny Joe said, referring to Chiun.

Remo handed the phone to Chiun. "It's for you."

"I am not deaf. Of course, it is for me. Who would waste time speaking with a son who fails to care for his aging father?"

"Blow it out your ears," Remo said, leaving the room.

"Hail to the Trainer who protects a tiny reservation in the desert of America."

"Morning, Chief," Sunny Joe said, ignoring the insult. "I have a favor to ask."

The sadness in Sunny Joe's voice caused Chiun to forego his usual bickering.

"What boon would you seek from the Master of Sinanju?"

Sunny Joe breathed in deeply. He knew that except for showing up at Freya's birthday parties, Chiun never did anything without being paid. Most of the time, overpaid.

"I've got a problem. My records keeper is dying."

"Surely he has trained another to carry on the tradition."

"Of course. But he wants to be buried in the Korean village. I was wanting to know if there was any way he could see Sinanju before he dies."

Chiun's eyes lit up and a smile stretched across his thin face.

"How glorious a day this is! This very morning, I was thinking how lovely it would be to return to my village! It has been too long since I have seen our glorious shores! I shall make this a death trip that shall be remembered for years to come!"

"He doesn't have long."

"Nonsense," Chiun said. "Unless the wretch has stopped breathing, he will live to see the beautiful shores of Sinanju!"

"It's not gonna be easy. Seems there's some kind of problem in North Korea."

"There is always a problem between whites and the House of Kim, but they will greet the House of Sinanju with open arms. Prepare your servant for his trip. The Master of Sinanju will arrive this very evening!"

Chiun dropped the phone on the floor and clapped his hands twice.

"I'm not a clapper device," Remo said. "And I have no idea how you're gonna get Smitty to approve a submarine trip to North Korea when we're nearly at war."

"Submarine?" Chiun asked, surprised. "This is no time to skulk about like cuttlefish! We shall arrive at the House of Kim in a private jet."

Remo shook his head and walked back into the kitchen. It was going to be another one of those days.

CHAPTER SIX

Ben Cole zipped up his parka and took a deep breath before opening a door out of his office. The ensuing blast of cold air destroyed the illusion that he had been sitting in the Oval Office. Ben entered quickly closed the door behind him to begin his monthly inspection of the supercomputers housed in his bunker.

The bunker was one of eight that had been constructed in the eighties, and one of dozens more that had been designed as a remote office for the President in case of nuclear attack. The bunker Ben's office was housed in was called the 'Arch Bunker' because of its proximity to St. Louis. It was modeled after the Oval Office, circa 1986, and, on paper, had been destroyed years earlier and flooded with concrete with the other seven of the era.

In reality, that was when his bunker was used for the first time. A lemony New Englander chose Cole — a former sleeper agent for Mossad — for an impossible job. Ben was to use all of the resources at his disposal to protect the United States from terrorists.

Ben inserted a flash drive into the first of the four computers stored in the sub-zero facility. He had named the refrigerator-sized computer Aleph. After Ben pressed his hand on the plate at the side of the keyboard and entered a code, the computer took itself offline for diagnostics. Ben retrieved the flash drive and moved to the second computer, Beth. He had no sooner inserted the drive when Aleph began beeping.

It was the first time the alarm had ever sounded. Since the four computers processed every scrap of information passing through North America, if any of his systems were compromised, it was automatically considered a national emergency.

Ben entered his authorization code and studied the output. It was a tiny blip, but enough to trigger security. A piece of malware had inserted itself, and though it had been quickly neutralized, it still had time to send a small coded message. Ben pulled up the terminal and his fingers moved across the keyboard with purpose. He copied the original file that had been downloaded — a benign report from an FBI branch in Lufkin, Texas — and isolated it to a specific location on one of Aleph's drives. He ran the code and monitored the output.

Hidden inside the code was a tiny file, only containing the IP address of Ben's primary computer. The path it took was what caught Ben's attention. It appeared to bounce across dozens of differing networks, only to return to Ben's location, as if one of his other computers was the source of the infection.

It took almost an hour for Ben to trace the file's complete path, and while it appeared that his first conclusion was correct, there was one anomaly: none of the other computers had received the data.

The only copy of his computers belonged to his employer, and those computers already knew his location. His phone rang and he set aside the questions that were building. Ben entered his office and shut the door behind him. Even though the air leaking from the server room had dropped the temperature of his office by twelve degrees, it felt abnormally warm. He tossed his parka on a chair and answered the phone.

"We've got trouble," Ben answered.

"Did you receive a call earlier today from Mr. Roam?" the lemony voice on the other end asked.

"Yes. He wanted me to send someone to North Korea."

"And that is what you are going to do," Smith said.

"Pardon?"

"Normally, we would not think to upset the political tension in Korea, but Master Chiun has exercised an old clause in our contract that deals with impending deaths in his family."

"Sunny Joe just said that his friend was sick."

"As you know, the members of the Arizona tribe are direct descendants of one of Chiun's ancestors. So, you will arrange travel for the Master of Sinanju and two…guests to fly to Seoul and then arrange for them to take a private jet to the capital of North Korea, Pyongyang."

"Wait…Pyongyang? We're almost at war."

"Agent Cole, one of the reasons you were specifically chosen for this job was because of your ability to make things happen. Granted, I would normally be the one making such arrangements, but another situation demands my attention," Smith said, sounding like a teacher who was disappointed when a student scored an A-.

"Besides, you will need to learn how to accommodate certain challenges that Masters of Sinanju provide from time to time."

"You're saying that I should have told Sunny Joe 'yes?'"

"That is exactly what I am saying."

During Ben's time with the Mossad, he had been taught that Sinanju was a mythical influence in the world. When he was first given command of his bunker and told he would only have one agent, he thought the idea was crazy — until he shot six rounds at Stone at point-blank range. The ex-Navy SEAL dodged each bullet with a smile on his face. When Smith ordered him to also take Stone's young sister onboard, Ben suddenly had his hands filled with problems on both sides of the keyboard.

"I can get them to Seoul, but I have no idea how you expect me to book them on a private jet to North Korea…not in this political environment."

"Regardless of the current political situation, both the Republic of Korea and their northern counterparts always accept requests from the Master of Sinanju."

Ben glanced at the monitors dedicated to monitoring North Korean activity.

"Is there a way to manipulate that channel to our benefit?"

"You will not find a soul on either side of the 38th parallel that will risk the direct wrath of the Master of Sinanju, nor will you find one here," Smith said.

"Okay, fine. I'll make it happen. But we have a bigger problem. Someone's tagged one of our computers. I think we've been compromised."

There was a pause on the other end.

"What have you found?" Smith asked, concern creeping into his voice.

"Not much yet. The odd thing is that it seemed to send the tag back to our computers."

"Have you completed a full security analysis?"

"I was just starting when you called," Ben said. "This is very…"

"We do not deal with speculations, Mr. Cole. Contact me when you have completed your analysis," Smith said and hung up.

"Dammit," Ben cursed.

He opened a hand-carved bone humidor on the edge of his desk. He had saved the cigars for times of exceptional pressure and this was one of them. They had been given to him as a perverse gesture of respect from the first enemy he had made after taking charge of the installation. And while Ben had once believed that Helmut Belisis — the head of a worldwide cabal named VIGIL — had died in an attack on his headquarters, he discovered that Helmut was alive and well, and still in command of what remained of the VIGIL network.

Ben pulled a cigar from the box and clipped the end. Even though the majority of the cigars remained, he noted the growing hole where the first two cigars had been. He lit the cigar, puffing slowly. One of the benefits of being the only person in your department was that you were able to assign smoking areas. His office was the sole designated smoking area.

Ben began searching for the contact information for the President of South Korea, but he could not get his mind off the possibility that his computers had been compromised. The trace showed that the file had returned to his own computers, but it was not there. It was almost as if a mirrored copy of his computers existed elsewhere and the only other copy of those computers belonged to Smith. *Was this another test?*

Ben took a puff from his cigar and considered the implications. Smith was too strict with the data they had to play games. Smith once begrudgingly admitted to having a backup of his computers, but would not tell Ben where the backup computers were located.

After setting up travel plans to North Korea, Ben would scour his computers until he found the loose end. And then he would have a talk with Smith.

CHAPTER SEVEN

Sunny Joe waited patiently on the roof of the Douglas hospital. Three men clad in dark jackets stood beside him on the helipad, each holding a large black case. The tallest of the men wore a small hat. The back of his right hand was covered by a tattoo of the name *MAC* crossed with swords.

"How much longer do we have to wait?" Mac asked, wiping his brow. "It's hot up here."

"He's 'fashionably late,' as usual," Sunny Joe said. "I was hoping this time he'd understand the gravity of the situation."

"Master of Sinanju or not, if he ain't here soon, I'm gone."

"Give it a minute, Mac. I need you."

Closing his eyes, Sunny Joe began searching with his ears, ignoring the traffic from the nearby airport, until he heard the sound of a helicopter in the distance.

"Get ready, boys. He's coming."

The three men reached down and opened their cases, taking out brightly colored guitars.

"You know that you're gonna have to eventually learn some Korean music."

Mac rolled his eyes. "We play mariachi music. Sue us."

"One song, that's all I ask," Sunny Joe said.

"You know, I'm glad you don't expect this every time you come home."

"Me, too," Sunny Joe said as the helicopter became visible in the northern sky.

"Fire it up," Mac said and the sound of mariachi music filled the helicopter pad.

The Master of Sinanju looked out the helicopter window and the smile on his wizened face disappeared.

"Why does the trainer have so few people here to greet me?" Chiun asked the pilot.

"I'm not supposed to speak with you, sir," the pilot said as the helicopter landed on the helipad. The blades tilted back and began slowing. "You're clear to go."

Chiun did not move.

"We've landed, sir," the pilot repeated. "You can go."

Chiun glanced at the door and smiled.

The pilot mumbled a curse and opened the door. Chiun exited, smiling and waving as if arriving at a rock concert. The band continued playing mariachi tunes until he stepped toward Sunny Joe and gave the slightest of bows.

"Hail to the Master of Sinanju," Sunny Joe said, deeply bowing in the traditional greeting of the Master. "He who sustains the village, faithfully keeps the code, and graciously throttles the universe."

"All is well, Trainer," Chiun said as he looked around the roof. "Where is your scribe?"

"He's still in his hospital bed. I thought you'd want to take a look at him first."

"And I thought I would be properly received as a Master of Sinanju," Chiun said, sighing. "Disappointment abounds for both of us this day."

Sunny Joe grimaced as he led Chiun to the hospital room where Mick was staying. Both he and Chiun traced their roots to a Master of Sinanju named Nonga; the only Master in Sinanju history to bear twin sons. Since Sinanju only permits one Master per generation, Nonga's twin son Kojong left to seek his fate across the Great Eastern Sea. He landed in California and traveled east, until he found a small tribe who welcomed him. After their chief and his eldest son were killed in battle, the tribe chose Kojong as their next chief.

As Kojong's descendant, Sunny Joe was the current chief of the Sinanju tribe. He had somehow gotten off on the wrong foot when he first met Chiun. Sunny Joe did not want to call himself a Master and challenge Chiun's role, so he simply referred to himself as a teacher. It soon became obvious that "Teacher" was a title Chiun had claimed exclusively, and ever since, he went out of his way to call Sunny Joe 'Trainer.'"

Chiun entered Mick's hospital room and upon seeing Freya, immediately smiled.

"Grandfather!" Freya said, returning the smile.

"Ah, my beautiful, young Freya," Chiun said and then mocked a frown as he touched her long, golden hair. "I see you have not reconsidered my proposal to change your hair to a more respectable color."

"Grandfather, my hair is gold, as was my mother's. I would not dishonor her memory."

"A pity," Chiun said, turning his gaze to Stone. "My granddaughter's sole weakness is my grandson's sole strength."

Stone rolled his eyes.

"Chief?" Sunny Joe asked, nodding toward Mick, who was hooked up to multiple lines and machines.

"No, this will not do," Chiun frowned, tearing the lines from the machines.

The instant that the machine's alarms began to blare, Chiun extended an impossibly-long fingernail into the front panel and silenced the device. The noise was enough to startle Mick awake. He looked around with weary eyes. Recognizing Chiun, he smiled and closed his eyes again.

Chiun leaned over Mick and prodded his body with his fingers, sniffing the air around him. "Your scribe shall live to see the glory that is Sinanju," Chiun said.

"Good," Sunny Joe said, smiling for the first time since Chiun arrived.

"Bring him to the whirlbird," Chiun said and then turned toward Freya and Stone.

"It is our tradition that a Master of Sinanju be accompanied by his pupil upon return to the village. But your father is more worried about the piece of paper that governs this country than the requests of his aged adoptive father. Therefore, I shall require one of you."

Stone glanced at the floor and placed his hands in his pocket. He did not have to wait to hear the name "Freya" come out of Chiun's mouth. She wasn't just his granddaughter; she was the jewel of his eye — the perfect child who could do no wrong. All he ever heard from Chiun was how great Freya was. How much she…

"Stone Smith, you shall escort me to the village," Chiun said dramatically.

"Me?" Stone asked, looking back and forth between Chiun and Freya.

"Is there another person who refers to himself as a rock in this room?" Chiun asked.

"Yes!" Stone yelled, sticking his tongue out at Freya. "He chose me!"

Sunny Joe grabbed Stone by the shoulder and twisted. The air went out of his lungs.

"This is a hospital."

"Sorry," Stone wheezed.

"Bring the scribe. I shall await you in the whirlbird," Chiun said, dramatically twirling so that the bottom edge of his kimono swirled behind him.

Kathleen leaned over Mick. She could tell that he was partially conscious.

"Keep your eyes closed," she said. "I know you can hear me."

Mick stirred and his eyes slid partially open.

"You are so stubborn," she said and gave him a kiss. "I don't want you to go, but I know why you have to."

"Somehow, someday, I want you to visit my resting spot," Mick whispered.

Kathleen leaned over and gave Mick a long hug. "I love you, Mr. Walker."

Mick smiled through a flash of pain. "I have…always loved you."

Kathleen stepped back toward Freya, allowing Sunny Joe and Stone to place Mick into a wheelchair. Sunny Joe glanced at Kathleen and then at Mick.

"My pop warned me that this day would come, but I never thought I'd see it."

"Victor…he knows where the…" Mick began and then surrendered to a coughing fit.

"Hush," Sunny Joe said. "This ain't time to talk about work."

Sunny Joe pushed Mick out of the room and led him to the elevator.

"Watch over Kathleen," Mick whispered.

"You don't have to ask," Sunny Joe said. "She's family."

Stone entered the elevator last and, seeing tears forming in his grandfather's eyes, looked away. The elevator trip was silent until they reached the roof. Mick motioned for Sunny Joe to come close.

"You gotta work with Paul," Mick said. "I've been…trying to help you work together. Sunny Joe, the tribe depends on it."

"Now, Mick…" Sunny Joe said, his voice trailing off.

Mick watched Sunny Joe's internal battle. Paul was head of the tribal council and he and Sunny Joe fought about everything. For the briefest of moments, Mick considered telling Sunny Joe that Paul was his half-brother, but it was a secret he had sworn to take to the grave.

Sunny Joe's expression softened and the moment passed.

"I'll try," was all that Sunny Joe would say.

"Thanks, Sunny Joe."

The helicopter sat on the helipad. Sunny Joe took one last look at Mick.

"Goodbye, old friend. I hope your path is a peaceful one," he said, reaching his arms around Mick. With the exception of the aged hazel eyes that were following Sunny Joe's every move, it appeared that Sunny Joe was giving his friend one last hug. But Chiun knew better. Sunny Joe reached around Mick's back, manipulating the core nerves throughout his spine. Mick collapsed in his chair and his breathing eased.

"That'll help you rest during the trip," Sunny Joe said, stepping back.

Stone loaded Mick's wheelchair into the helicopter and secured it in the back. He nodded goodbye to Sunny Joe and sat by Chiun. As the helicopter lifted off, Sunny Joe stood still, watching his friend leave for the last time.

"There are certain duties that accompany the position of pupil," Chiun said.

"To be honest, I was surprised that you chose me," Stone said, smiling. "Thanks."

"It is a tradition to bring a pupil and, despite what you may have been taught to the contrary, Sinanju lives by tradition."

"Well, whatever you need, I'm your man," Stone said proudly.

"Excellent," Chiun said. "As soon as we land at the airport, my steamer trunks will need to be transported to the plane."

"Trunks? What trunks?"

"I packed light," Chiun said, nodding toward the back. "There are only eight."

Stone looked behind Mick. While he had noticed the stack of ancient wooden steamer trunks when he secured Mick, he had not thought anything about them.

"Wait, all of those are yours?"

Chiun smiled.

"Oh, okay, now I get it. *That's* why you didn't choose Freya! You just needed me to carry your luggage!"

"And what an honor it is, apprentice pupil to a trainer of Sinanju."

Stone glared at Chiun. "So, what's our itinerary?"

"We will visit the village of your ancestors, but first, we must stop in Pyongyang."

"Pyong…you mean we're going to the capital of North Korea? They'll eat us alive!"

"A paper tiger is only fearsome to those afraid of paper."

"That idiot has nukes!"

"There is no need to worry," Chiun said. "Nook is a common name."

The helicopter took them to Douglas airport, landing near the edge of the runway. Stone's eyes opened wide as he saw Captain Hammond in his trademark baseball cap, sitting on a lawn chair in front of his rundown plane. Stone had forgotten that Ben had placed the retired fighter pilot on retainer in case they needed an emergency flight. Hammond was as mean and crusty as anyone Stone had ever come in contact with in the military, and he did not imagine that Chiun would put up with any of his crap.

"Uh, you're probably going to want me to go ahead and talk to…"

Chiun held up one hand.

"Care for the transportation of my trunks. And the scribe."

The helicopter pilot held the door open for him, and Chiun glided toward Captain Hammond. Stone unfastened Mick from the harnesses as quickly as he could and glanced back outside. Remembering his last encounter with Captain Hammond, Stone hurried to get Mick out of the helicopter. Once on the ground, Stone took a quick look at Mick, who was still asleep.

"Sorry Mick, we've got to move," Stone said, racing Mick toward the plane.

But he was too late. Captain Hammond stood, removed his worn baseball cap and faced Chiun.

This is going to be messy, Stone thought, involuntarily wincing. He wondered how he was going to explain to Cole what had happened to Captain Hammond.

As Chiun came within striking range, Captain Hammond gave a low bow.

"All Hail the Master of Sinanju," he said, stepping out of Chiun's way.

"Speed us to the city of the Franciscan Saints," Chiun said, entering the plane.

Stone caught up to Captain Hammond just as he tucked the lawn chair under his arm.

"What are you lookin' at, moron?" Hammond asked. "Get that man onboard and load that luggage! The Master of Sinanju is waiting for you."

CHAPTER EIGHT

Kathleen placed her hand on the bed where Mick had been laying and closed her eyes. The sheets were still warm from his body heat. Though she had known for months that his time was growing short, the empty bed in front of her still seemed unreal.

"A part of him will always be with you," Freya said softly.

"That's why I didn't want to go to the roof," Kathleen said. "I know it sounds stupid, but as long as I didn't actually see him leave on the helicopter…as long as my last sight is seeing Sunny Joe wheel him out of the room, part of me that believes he will come back."

Kathleen wiped away the tears building up.

"Let's get out of here," Kathleen said, grabbing her purse.

Freya followed her and silently entered Kathleen's car.

"Mr. Mick loves you more than anything."

"Yes, he does. And I have no idea what they had to do to get him to North Korea, but I'm glad they did," she said, wiping away tears. "I really am."

"I have only been to the Korean homeland once. He will be happy."

"That's all Mick ever talked about. Well, and you."

"What did he mean when he said that he saw me as a bridge?"

Kathleen smiled. "He sees you as the embodiment of both the House and the Tribe. He said that you'll be the person to reunite us with the homeland."

"I don't know how I can do that," Freya said. "But I am glad that he thinks well of me."

The artificial environment of the city surrendered to the southeastern Arizona desert once they passed the Douglas city limits. Kathleen headed east toward the reservation.

"A lot of people talk about you," Kathleen said. "And even though most of us don't like our current situation and everyone dreams of being reunited with the Korean House, no one seems to want to change."

"Change is a part of life," Freya said. "Whether good or bad."

Kathleen parked her emotions for a moment and looked at Freya. Her childhood had been spent travelling throughout Europe until her mother was murdered. Only a miracle reunited Freya with her father, who had to leave her with her paternal grandfather Sunny Joe.

"You've been through quite a bit for someone your age," Kathleen said. "You've already seen enough death for a lifetime."

"There is nothing to say. Life has many shades, and the final shade is death. One day, I shall be reunited with my Mother in the Halls of Valhalla."

"I never thought to ask if you were religious," Kathleen said.

"It is not something I speak about," Freya said. "Tell me something about Mr. Mick that I don't know."

Kathleen thought for a moment and then smiled.

"You look at them now and you only see the best of friends, but he and Billy were something of an arranged marriage at first."

"What do you mean?" Freya asked.

"Well, Mick's father was the records keeper for Billy's father," Kathleen explained. Freya knew that she was the only one who got away with calling Sunny Joe 'Billy.' "And since Mick was the only boy in the family, it was expected that he would end up working for Billy. They were set up to play together right after Mick was born. Oh, how they used to fight."

Kathleen's smile disappeared.

"Billy's father was mean. I don't think I ever saw that man smile, not once. And he trained Billy hard."

Freya subconsciously looked down. Sunny Joe had privately confided in her that his father had committed suicide. "Did Mick know him?"

The sadness in Kathleen's eyes was replaced with a spark of anger.

"Mick's father died a few years before Billy returned, so Mick took over keeping records for Billy's father. Sometimes, he would come home with unexplained back pains. Once, he came home with a broken wrist. Oh, he tried to explain it away. He said that he fell, or some nonsense, but he couldn't fool me; I'm a nurse. The break was too clean, almost as if something broke the bones from the inside."

"I am sorry," Freya said, recognizing the description of a ghost stroke.

"When he died unexpectedly, I was happy. Mick said that was wrong, but I could tell that he was relieved, too.

"I guess we're lucky Grandfather is the way he is."

"You have no idea," Kathleen said. "For a trainee of Sinanju, Billy grew up pretty shy."

"I gather that you used to like each other?" Freya said and then leaned back. "I am sorry, I did not mean to infer…"

"Billy and I, well, we had our time to flirt, but when it came to Dawn? I never stood a chance. He loved that woman."

Tears began to well up again and Kathleen wiped her eyes.

"When they told us that Dawn died in childbirth, we had no idea the baby survived. The first time I saw Remo, your dad, I know he could tell I was staring, but I couldn't help it. I just felt terrible that he grew up not knowing that he had a family."

"But he has one now," Freya said. "Though I do wish he would see us more often."

"I don't think he feels at home anywhere," Kathleen said. "He leads a hard life."

Kathleen pulled onto the road leading to the reservation. The rundown Sinanju Motel stood at the edge of the highway, a bleached strip of mostly unused rooms.

"That's where Tekoa is staying," Freya said, smiling.

Kathleen's eyes hardened. While most of the tribe had been won over by the polite stranger, she still had questions. Tekoa said that he had been banished from a tribe in East Texas. When asked why, he explained that he was the sole survivor of a car crash with his parents and the tribe considered him cursed. He spent the first few months of his stay working hard and petitioned the council to become a member of the Tribe against

Sunny Joe's wishes. After he became a member of the tribe, there was nothing Sunny Joe could do.

"You need to be careful about that boy," she said. "Don't ever tell Billy I said this, but if he says something is true, I believe him. If he says we need to worry about that boy, then something's wrong."

"Tekoa has always been nice to me," Freya said defensively. "When the other boys make fun of me, he always defends me."

"Listen to me, Freya. You've experienced a lot of parts of life, but you're still young. And I'm sorry to say that you're probably going to find a lot more darkness…especially in your line of work."

Freya sat back in her seat and crossed her arms. Tekoa was the best thing to happen since she arrived. Kathleen just didn't understand.

CHAPTER NINE

McCabe struggled to pull what looked like a human body out of his trunk and into the building.

"What are you doing?" Zelensky asked as McCabe grunted his way inside the lab.

"I brought it from the house," McCabe explained as he laid the object on the floor. He unrolled the blanket, revealing a lifelike sex doll. Its shiny eyes stared mindlessly at the ceiling.

"But why *that*?" Zelensky asked.

"The mannequin's plastic is cracking from age, so I figured we could use this until we get funding for proper skin. It's a large doll, so it should fit."

Zelensky stared at the buxom doll. It was life-sized and anatomically correct, with red hair and blue eyes. Permanent red lipstick highlighted an empty smile.

"What are we supposed to do with it?" Zelensky asked.

"We take the old plastic off Smirnoff then take one limb at a time from Becky. We'll attach them separately so we have as few seams as possible."

"Becky?" Zelensky asked, smiling. "You named that thing?"

"Well, I had to call her something."

"Wait, didn't you tell me that your first girlfriend was named Becky?"

McCabe's face flushed red.

"We start with the torso and then add limbs," McCabe said, changing the subject. "I've got some sealant that should hold everything together."

"Becky had red hair, too, didn't she?"

"Will you shut up and help me?"

Zelensky looked down at the human figure and sneered.

"You realize how creepy this is, don't you?" he said. "I'm not skinning 'Becky'! You do it."

"Fine," McCabe said. "Do you have a knife?"

"I'm going to pretend that you didn't say that," Zelensky said. "While you were off playing with dolls, I gave Smirnoff a full mechanical rundown."

"Did you find out about that weird metal on her chest and head?" McCabe asked. "I can't figure out what it is."

Zelensky knew all about Orichalcum. It was a rare hybrid that existed outside of the periodic table; light as aluminum and stronger than diamond. He knew that it was ordered by Helmut to provide Smirnoff with superior armor. He also knew that it was more expensive than platinum, so even Helmut was forced to limit her plating to critical areas. But McCabe did not need to know that.

"It's probably just a messed-up batch of aluminum."

"Someone should really patent it," McCabe said. "I can't put a dent in it."

"Why were you trying to dent it?" Zelensky asked.

"Just seeing what I could find out," McCabe said. "What did your rundown reveal?"

"The only weaknesses I found were in her sensors."

"What's wrong with them?"

"She has VCR-level optics, like from the nineties."

"You can fix that. Aren't you still friends with Midgley? He's got all the advanced stuff."

Zelensky stroked his chin. He did not want anyone else involved if possible, but he needed to do something to get back on Helmut's good side. His parents depended on his success.

"Good idea. I'll check on that."

McCabe removed a small panel in Smirnoff's stomach. He carefully inserted a small chip and began soldering wires to it.

"Wait, what are you doing?" Zelensky asked. While Helmut had not said anything about unauthorized modifications, he could not imagine it was something he would tolerate.

"Remember my Alpha Ray? I figured out how to implement it into her system!"

"Oh, God, not the Alpha Ray again."

"You promised that I could do use it," McCabe said.

"I thought you said that it only worked on geriatric mice."

"That was my low-powered version. This is much more powerful; it generates a low frequency pulse that should calm anyone within thirty feet of her. I designed it to broadcast if she ever feels threatened. We don't need a Mr. Gordons situation."

"Fine. I'll work out the power issues," Zelensky said. "You just finish your…skinning or whatever. I'm going home."

Zelensky ran out of the building to phone in his update and violently scrubbed his fingers through his hair. How had it come to this? At first, it was just a matter of money. Helmut offered Zelensky more money than he had ever seen in his life to work on a project. But as Zelensky learned more about the plan, he felt a pang of conscience, and told Helmut that he could no longer work with him.

Zelensky soon found himself on the bad side of the rich man with the fancy cane. The next morning, an envelope was slid under his door, filled with pictures of his parents being held at gunpoint. The large checks stopped coming, and Helmut's demands only increased. Helmut was showing him who was boss.

Thinking about his parents, Zelensky set his conscience aside and dialed the number.

CHAPTER TEN

The Incheon International Airport in Seoul was buzzing with activity. Ever since the North fired missiles crossing South Korean airspace, foreigners had scrambled to book flights out of the country. The sudden congestion caused the South to double its security, resulting in yet more delays.

Families began camping near their terminal so they would not be bumped from flights. Airports became so crowded that police were called in to clear paths for people to walk. The Red Cross had even set up stations to feed waiting families.

So when air traffic control was told to hold all flights for the passage of a private jet, the controllers refused. The President of South Korea had to personally call the head of security. He ordered all flights grounded pending the launch of a private jet. Not only would the jet be given priority to Korean airspace, no record of the flight would be logged at any level.

The Korean government had commandeered the luxury jet. It had been specially made for the Sultan of Brunei and parked in a private hanger, reserved for his personal use. The Sultan was furious until he was told who requested his plane. Shortly later, a large basket of dried fruit and flowers was delivered to the plane in a 24-karat gold-plated vase.

Two of South Korea's finest pilots entered the plane and performed pre-flight checks. The older pilot was a colonel in the Korean Air Force with twenty years' experience. The younger man was a captain, known to be South Korea's best fighter pilot. Every form of identification had been removed from the men, but they knew each other by reputation.

"What do you think the odds are that we survive?" the captain asked.

"Blasted out of the sky or nuked, what does it matter?" the colonel replied.

"True," the captain said. "This assignment is off the books. No one would ever know if we were shot down over North Korean airspace."

"For what it's worth, the President told me that we were the safest people in the peninsula. I assume this is a last-moment diplomatic outreach."

"That's what I thought, until I saw the steamer trunks," the captain whispered nervously. "At first, I thought they were Chinese because of the hand-carved symbols, but I looked closer. The symbols were gold. Real gold."

Both men knew what that meant.

"The Master does live in a western province of North Korea," the colonel said. "Would he involve himself in political talks with the South?"

"No one has seen the Master in decades," the captain replied. "Perhaps the very fact that we are moving his trunks will be enough for the North to reconsider their actions."

The younger pilot stood and glanced out the small, bulletproof window that separated them from the cabin. A young white American was pushing an older man in a wheelchair, but the captain could tell he was not the Master. Then he saw the old man seated in the Monarch's portable throne. He was Korean and very old. His bright sapphire kimono was striped with golden filigree.

"Check the camera," the captain said, gulping. "I think the Master is onboard."

The colonel flipped his monitor to one of the cabin cameras. Chiun waved and smiled at him. He turned the monitor off.

"I think we need to stop talking," the colonel said. "This is way above our paygrade."

The younger pilot clenched his jaw and stared straight ahead.

"They know how to spend money," Stone said, looking at the jet's interior. If he had not seen the windows, he would have thought they were being seated in a luxurious office.

"Did you load my trunks?" Chiun asked.

"Yeah," Stone said. "Why are they so heavy?"

"Quality products are heavy. Secure the scribe," Chiun barked. "I must find the lavatory."

"Fine with me," Stone said.

Chiun headed to the back as Stone fastened Mick's wheelchair to the cargo latches at the front of the plane. Whatever Sunny Joe had done had kept him asleep during the flight over the Pacific. Stone looked toward the back. On the long flight over, there was nowhere to smoke without Chiun knowing.

After Chiun returned, Stone would excuse himself and take a quick smoke break. But when he checked his pockets, nothing was there. He had just bought a pack of cigarettes before they left. *Where were they?*

He heard the toilet flush. Stone squinted his eyes shut in frustration as Chiun returned from the restroom smiling.

"Dammit, Chiun! You took my cigarettes!"

"Did your trainer not teach you that cursing is a form of helplessness?"

"Yeah, yeah, Sunny Joe's already scolded me about 'wasted breath.'"

"Secondly, you may refer to me as Master Chiun. In fact, since I am your spiritual grandfather, you may address me as Grandmaster Chiun."

Stone began nervously tapping his foot as he glared at Chiun.

"I really needed those cigarettes, Chi…"

"Grandmaster Chiun."

"Fine. Grandmaster Chiun, that was my only pack of cigarettes!"

"Thank you for letting me know. Now I can travel without having to hold my nose. It is bad enough that I have to endure your breath. Has your gullet no shame?"

Stone found a seat across from Chiun and crossed his arms. As the plane began taxiing down the runway, Stone noticed that Chiun was intently staring at something out the window.

"What's wrong?"

"If you watch the wings, they bend while in flight. If they are to detach, I wish to know."

"Oh, I think we'll all know if a wing breaks off."

"One can never tell with a Canadian airplane," Chiun replied. "The slightest bit of French influence weakens the design."

Stone stared at Chiun. To an ordinary observer, he looked like a frail, hundred-year-old man. Stone knew that was what he wanted people to think. Beneath the thin, wrinkled skin and the feigned weakness existed the deadliest man to walk the Earth. And that scared Stone more than his body desired cigarettes. Sunny Joe spoke of him as the true Master of Sinanju. Maybe he could teach Stone how Sunny Joe punched through the pane with his finger.

"Chi...Grandmaster Chiun, can you punch holes through glass?"

A puzzled look came across Chiun's face.

"What sort of question is this? A child can punch a hole through glass. It is very fragile."

"No, I mean can you punch a hole through glass so it doesn't leave cracks?"

Chiun looked even more confused.

"What is Remo's father teaching you? I was led to believe that he was teaching you and my fair Freya a form of Sinanju."

Stone turned his head as he heard a cough. Mick blinked a couple of times and opened his eyes.

"Where are we?" he asked.

"Why don't you tell him, Grandmaster Chiun?" Stone asked, smirking.

"We are headed to the glorious village of Sinanju, the land of your ancestors," Chiun said proudly. "Perhaps we will even have time to find a proper Korean wife for this one."

"Whoa, I don't think so," Stone said, waving his hands.

"You do not fool me, son of Remo Williams," Chiun said, wagging his finger. "You are a harlot. I will be watching to make sure you do not deflower any of the fair maidens of Sinanju."

Stone smirked. Maybe he would find a way to enjoy this trip after all.

"First, we must stop in Pyongyang, the glorious capitol of our homeland."

"What?" Mick asked with a start. "But why?"

"It is a surprise," Chiun whispered, leaning forward. "A gift from the People's Republic of Korea to the second-best caretaker in the world."

"The second-best…what are you talking about?"

"Thank you for your concern. This trip is not just about you," Chiun said. "We will also meet with the young Kim. He has not seen me since he was a child and I wish to remind him of his family's arrangement with Sinanju."

"Wait, you're taking us to see Kim?" Stone asked.

"Shhh, it's part of the surprise," Chiun said, nodding toward Mick. "Now, let an old man get some sleep."

Stone heard snoring as soon as Chiun laid his head back. Very loud snoring.

"Stone, what's he got us into?" Mick asked. "I just want to be buried in the village — and maybe even see it, if I can make it in time."

"I'm just the cheap white help," Stone said. "Are you feeling any better?"

"Sunny Joe did something to my back so that I can't feel pain, but I can still feel the pressure behind the pain. My heart's pounding really hard."

"Grandpa knows what he's doing."

"I sure hope that *he* does," Mick said, nodding toward Chiun.

"Chiun got us into this, so he's going to get us out," Stone said. "The flight's about an hour and a half. I'm going to get some rest before we land."

"But I just woke up," Mick grumbled.

"Have fun," Stone said, leaning his plush seat all the way back. The sound of the engines soon became a soothing *whoosh* as he began wondering what the village of Sinanju was actually like. Between all the stories that Sunny Joe and Mick had told him, he could picture it in his mind.

Stone opened his eyes. He stood at the top of an icy hill, between two huge stone outcroppings, the 'Horns of Welcome' that Mick had told him about. Stone looked at the seventy-foot-tall pillars and shook his head. Mick had told him with a straight face that they had been hand-carved by a past Master of Sinanju.

He bristled at the bitter wind and looked back over the Western Korean Sea. In the distance, he could see a few small islands to the northwest, but despite all of the build-up, Stone was not impressed. He only saw a cold, muddy landscape. Even the sea appeared a dead and cold gray.

Then he heard a whisper.

당신은 선택되었습니다, 주 님 ⊠⊠

At first, he was confused by the voice, which spoke in Korean. *What did it say?* 'Chosen Lord'? Stone looked around, trying to find the source of the whisper, wondering how he could even hear it in the howling wind.

Dangsin-eun siantaeg doesseubniba, ju nim Shinan

'The Chosen Lord Sinan'? That made no sense. Stone looked up. The voice was coming from the top of the Horn to his right. For a moment, Stone thought to find Chiun, but then imagined how foolish he would look telling the Master of Sinanju that one of the Horns was speaking to him.

Stone looked around to ensure no one was watching and began scaling the Horn. By Mick's description of the Horns back at the reservation, Stone thought that they would be majestic, smoothly-carved obelisks. But as he scaled the pillar, he saw weathered strokes, as if the Horns had been carved with something like an axe. Stone kept to the west side, so no one would see him ascend.

He was surprised when he reached the top. It came to a much more jagged point than appeared from the ground. A small pocket had been carved out on the far side. The voice whispered again, and Stone almost lost his grip.

Dangsin-eun siantaeg doesseubniba, ju nim Shinan

Stone peered into the small indention and saw a skull. It had been partially worn down by the elements, but something had kept it mounted in place. As he looked closer, he saw a glint of light behind the skull, so he tried to reach around it.

The skull turned toward him, and a dark light filled the eye sockets as a voice filled his mind.

DANGSIN-EUN SIANTAEG DOESSEUBNIBA, JU NIM SHINAN!

Stone lost his grip, falling back from the Horn. He was too far out to reach the rock and too high to land on his feet. He twisted his body to prepare for impact.

Stone was startled awake when the jet hit an air pocket. As he tried to gain his bearings, he heard a new sound; the subtle whine of high-powered jets. Glancing out the window, he saw North Korean fighter jets flying on both sides of their plane.

"Chiun!" he bellowed. "Out the window!"

Chiun arched his back slowly as if coming from a coma and glanced at the wing. It was slightly shaking, so he began counting bolts to make sure they had all remained.

"The wing is secure," Chiun said, leaning his head back to sleep.

"Wing? What? Don't you see the jets?"

"Escorts," Chiun said, casually waving his hand. "They will ensure our safe arrival to meet their Glorious Leader."

Stone nervously watched the jets flying within a hundred feet from where he was sitting and took a deep breath.

I really need a cigarette, he thought.

CHAPTER ELEVEN

The Supreme leader of the Democratic People's Republic of Korea paced nervously around the People's Palace. His military advisors had warned him that there had been rumors of America sending SEAL teams to take him out. Despite his public proclamations otherwise, he knew that his guards were not ready to engage highly-trained American forces. The idiots would probably let them through in exchange for a cheeseburger.

The burden of being Supreme Leader had been thrust upon Kim at a young age. When his father died, he was immediately placed at center stage. Though not the eldest son, he was the favored son — not of his father, who personally disliked him, but of his grandfather. And no one questioned the man who had won independence for the North and provided America with their first military stalemate.

Finding his way to an ornately-armored door at the end of a long and luxurious hallway, Kim straightened his jacket and opened the door. Holding his multiple chins high, he entered the room.

His heel clicks echoed in the silence of the enormous room. Generals sat around a large table in the center of the room, while the walls were manned by an armed contingent of young captains. Each man had sworn to sacrifice his own life to protect him if the Americans attacked.

As one, the room came to attention and each man produced the kind of smooth salute that is only possible by practicing in a mirror. They did not salute their leader for honor or for sharing time in the battle field. They saluted because it was an order given, and because they knew that Kim had fed his own uncle to wild dogs for daring to yawn during one of his speeches.

Kim looked around, as if to study the angle of each man's hand, and then returned the salute. The generals seated themselves, flashing practiced smiles.

Before he could sit at the head of the table, the door burst open. Kim flinched before recognizing the man who ran into the room — his cousin Ug.

"Supreme Leader!" Ug shouted. "I have urgent news!"

Kim glared at him. Embarrassed that his generals saw him flinch, he stormed over to Ug.

"What can possibly be important enough to interrupt a meeting of the People's Glorious Council of Vengeance?" Kim sputtered.

"A jet is headed this way from the South!"

Kim crossed his arms and his eyes narrowed. His cousin was about three seconds from having a bullet between his eyes.

"And why has this plane been allowed to fly over our splendid lands?"

"I have standing orders to allow the Master of Sinanju access to any and all air space."

Officially, the Supreme Leader did not need to defecate. This was taught to all North Korean children as a fact. North Korean professors had written volumes boasting about the strength of the Supreme Leader's intestines. So it was only natural that his generals turned away as one, for they did not want to disrespect the Supreme Leader by acknowledging that he had soiled his pants.

Captain Pak Moon Won scowled. An ambitious man since joining the army, he leaned toward his roommate, Woo Kee Win.

"Why does the Supreme Leader fear this old man?" Pak whispered. "If the Master of Sinanju is even still alive, he is old and weak."

"He has promoted myths that strike fear into our leader's heart," Woo whispered in reply. "It is time for someone to break his hold over our government."

Woo walked toward the Supreme Leader and saluted. Kim's guards raised their rifles.

"Supreme Leader, give the word and I shall execute this miscreant from Sinanju myself!" Woo shouted.

Kim turned toward the captain, his eyes still filled with terror.

"Are you insane?" Kim shouted, firing his pistol into Woo. He kept pulling the trigger, even after the chamber was empty.

As a young man, Kim had asked the same question to his grandfather. Until the Master of Sinanju announced his visit, young Kim had never seen a moment of weakness or fear in his grandfather. It angered young Kim when he saw his grandfather tremble in this man's presence.

"Grandfather, why do you allow this old man to speak to you like this? Rise and strike him down!"

Kim's grandfather, who loved his grandson more than anything in the world, slapped young Kim hard enough to knock him to the ground. Then he began kicking him until he was a pile of bruised sobs. His grandfather finally pulled Kim up. Kim had never seen such desperate fear in a person's eyes.

"Know this, young Kim. I may be the one true god, but your very life depends on knowing that there is only one true Master — the Master of Sinanju."

When Chiun later appeared to his grandfather, young Kim watched him carefully. He looked like a frail old man, dressed in a bright kimono. Kim turned in shock as a small army of his grandfather's soldiers jumped from the curtains, AK-47's blazing. Kim laughed as the man who caused his grandfather such fear was riddled with bullets.

As the bullets continued flying his way, the old man did not move; only a faint blurriness appeared around his small frame. The wall behind the Master exploded in puffs of stone as each bullet seemed to pass through him. The Master turned toward Kim and smiled, as if sharing a private joke.

After the men spent all of their bullets, they advanced as one to attack the Master. Kim had seen these men train. They were handpicked for their efficiency and cruelty. They surrounded the Master in a circle, knives drawn.

Young Kim felt the gentlest of breezes, and all of the men fell dead.

There were no marks on their bodies; there was no blood on the floor. But Kim could tell that life no longer inhabited the soldiers' bodies. The old man in the brightly-colored kimono smiled serenely. His grandfather immediately bowed before the old man, wailing and begging.

"Forgive me, oh Master," his grandfather pleaded. "These men acted on their own. Their families shall pay for their insubordination."

"You shall do them no harm," The Master said. "My wrath is saved for you and your family should our agreement be placed in question."

Then young Kim saw something that was hard to believe. His grandfather, the most powerful man in the world, knelt before the old man. And when he spoke, his voice was weak and devoid of emotion.

"All hail the Master of Sinanju," his grandfather said. "He who sustains the village, faithfully keeps the code and graciously throttles the universe."

Then Chiun turned his attention to young Kim. Though an old man, his sharp hazel eyes were full of energy. Kim's breaths came in shallow gasps as the Master of Sinanju knelt to his eye level.

"You now know this lesson, yes?" Chiun asked.

Kim squeaked in fear, nodding 'yes.'

"Good boy," Chiun said, patting him on the head.

Now a man himself, and in charge of the same country his grandfather had kept free from the evil Americans, Kim looked at the captain's body on the floor. The men around him were still smiling. "Clean this up!" he shouted.

The generals scrambled, taking off their jackets to soak up the blood. Others barked orders at the captains against the wall and pointed at the stains. Soon, the entire war room was full of military men on their knees wiping the floor with their jackets. Looking around the room, Kim nodded and left. After the door closed, the eldest general stood to his feet.

"You have shamed me!" he yelled at the captains. "One of my own dared raise his voice to the Supreme Leader! And worse, questioned the Master of Sinanju! You will all be punished!"

"Yes, sir!" the captains replied as one.

"This entire floor shall be spotless when I return! Then we prepare for the Master's visit!"

The generals peered out the door and, not seeing Kim, left the captains to clean the floor.

"This is madness," Pak said. "We are supposed to be the spear of the Glorious Leader's strike force…and we are forced to clean the floor on our knees, like maids!"

"It is not wise to speak thusly in the war room," another whispered. "The Supreme Leader has ears everywhere."

"Except Sinanju," Pak said, spitting on the floor. "How can we be held hostage by a tiny fishing village?"

"It is not safe to taunt the Master."

"If you wish to be safe, then become a farmer," Pak sneered. "I serve to conquer!"

"My father served Kim Il Sung himself. He saw the Master dodge bullets and render a tank asunder."

Pak stood to his feet. He left his jacket on the floor.

"Your father is a coward. The rest of you may remain chambermaids, but I refuse to kneel to an old man who threatens us with fairy tales. Who will stand with me?"

The captains looked at each other until one man stood.

"I stand with you!" Captain Cho Jin Soo said. "What do you propose?"

"An end to this farce," Pak said, a smile stretching across his face. "This trickery cannot be allowed to continue! Know this: whoever brings the head of the Master of Sinanju to our Supreme Leader will be greatly rewarded!"

A few of the other captains stood to their feet, cautiously listening.

"Good," Captain Pak said. "I see we have a few men in our midst. We will strike in two phases. I will lead the strike force to kill the Master here, while another will be sent to destroy the village of Sinanju."

"I will lead the attack on the village," Captain Cho said. "Eight men should be enough."

Pak smiled. The end of Sinanju was near.

CHAPTER TWELVE

Smirnoff walked around the laboratory. She compared it with the last time she had seen it when her original creator was making her. Two human males were in the room, Creator Randy McCabe and his subordinate. Both were busy at their computers. Smirnoff accessed the various greetings that were reserved in her programming. She changed her voice to a warm, feminine tone.

"Good morning, Vietnam! Hello is all right. Good evening, ladies and germs."

"The software's working," McCabe said victoriously.

"What is covering my frame?" Smirnoff asked. "It restricts my movements."

"Well, it's…it's like an artificial skin," McCabe said. "It makes you look more human."

"It is not fitted for either my size or my movements," Smirnoff said. She extended an arm and the rubber tore behind her shoulder. "This will not do."

"After we get some more funding, I bet we can…"

A low hum emanated from Smirnoff's center and the rubber

skin covering her began to break down into small particles of what looked like pink oatmeal. It smelt like burnt toast.

"What are you doing?" McCabe asked. "That cost four thousand dollars!"

"Acclimating the material for use," Smirnoff explained.

Smirnoff scrolled through a digital catalog of human faces and chose the most symmetrical. The clumps of flesh-toned oatmeal began jiggling and then the newly formed tissue settled, covering the entire surface of her body. Her face smoothed itself into perfect balance. She had a strong, thin nose sitting atop pouting lips, with high, sculpted cheekbones.

"How did you do that?" McCabe asked, holding her arm close to his face. "That's amazing! It looks just like human skin, right down to the pores!"

"Except for her eyes. They're just…flat," Zelensky said. "It's creeping me out."

McCabe turned to his desk and returned with a spare set of his blue-tinted contacts.

"I knew your eyes weren't really that blue!" Zelensky said.

"They're *mostly* blue. Hold still," McCabe said, placing the contacts over her eyes.

"That's better…but she still has no fingernails," Zelensky noted.

"Why do you have to be so nitpicky?" McCabe asked defensively. "We'll just buy her some of those fake nail things that everyone wears."

"Then maybe we can get her some Barbie clothes, and you can play Ken, and we'll have loads of fun!" Zelensky mocked.

"Now if this will only get our idiot bosses at NASA to stop breathing down our necks," McCabe said.

"Why do they breathe on your neck?" Smirnoff asked.

"It's a figure of speech," McCabe said. "They've been threatening to shut us down for months now."

"You are being threatened?" Smirnoff asked. "By whom?"

"Our NASA bosses," Zelensky said. "If we don't show them progress, they're going to fire us."

"Fire you?" Smirnoff asked.

"You know, terminate us," McCabe said.

Smirnoff created a new note: *NASA bosses wish to terminate Creator Randy McCabe.*

"This is the limit of my programming for approximating a human female given the parameters of my current situation," Smirnoff explained.

"You look perfect!" McCabe said and then looked down at the rest of her body. "*Too* perfect. Let me give you my lab coat."

"Are you kidding me?" Zelensky said. "She looks better than the original doll!"

McCabe ignored Zelensky and grabbed his lab coat, draping it over Smirnoff's shoulders. He fastened the three buttons in the center of the coat, which was barely long enough to cover the top of her thighs.

"What is the purpose of this garment?" Smirnoff asked.

"It covers up your, uh…" McCabe stuttered. "Y-y-your…"

"You can't even talk to her!" Zelensky started laughing. "Smirnoff, he doesn't want you to be naked."

As Smirnoff recognized one of the trigger words for foreplay, her personality changed.

"But I want him to see me naked," Smirnoff said, slowly removing the lab coat.

She walked toward McCabe, backing him against the wall and began to gently stroke his hair with her fingertips. "I am yours, Randy McCabe."

"That's my cue," Zelensky said, turning to the door.

"Wait, hold on! Don't leave!" McCabe said, shooing Smirnoff away.

Smirnoff grabbed him and pulled him close to her. "But did you not purchase this form so you could…"

"That was before!" McCabe interrupted. "Zelensky, you can't leave!"

"Have fun," Zelensky said. "I'll be back tomorrow." He made a mental note to leave this out of his report.

CHAPTER THIRTEEN

The Pentagon was called to High Alert after they detected the movements of three battalions of North Korean troops. Though tensions on the 38th Parallel were high, the Pentagon did not need to worry about the massive movement of one of the world's largest armies. They were not moving south to the DMZ. They were heading west to Pyongyang.

The soldiers had been scrambled by a last-minute order from the Supreme Leader himself: gather as many people as possible to line the People's Square in Pyongyang for a parade later that day. Normally, such arrangements took weeks to plan, especially with biting winter winds that kept most North Korean citizens huddled inside for warmth.

Today, thirty thousand citizens stood on each side of the paved road, carrying white and golden roses. Though hungry and cold, they were smiling real smiles for the first time in a very long time.

When the soldiers had appeared that morning, ordering them at gunpoint to attend a parade at Pyongyang Square, each family numbly gathered their warmest clothes and balls of cooked rice for the long, grueling day of screaming on cue. But when they found out that the Master of Sinanju would be in attendance for the ceremonies, families not only began to volunteer, they helped tell their neighbors.

Inside his palace, Kim stood near the door that led to the balcony where he would address the hastily-assembled crowd.

"It is my wish that you and your guest feel most honored," he said, bowing deeply.

Chiun peered out the window and sniffed. The crowds grew smaller each time he visited. Everywhere he went, it seemed that people had forgotten what it meant to greet a Master of Sinanju.

"Do you feel honored?" Kim asked with a hopeful smile.

"Three battalions are enough this time. We are, after all, only honoring an American," Chiun said as his eyes narrowed. "But I will expect a proper greeting next time."

Kim bowed and walked toward the balcony door. He made a mental note to shoot the general in charge of the parade. Taking a deep breath, Kim nodded and his guards opened the door. At the first flutter of movement, the crowd exploded in shouts and applause. Every person gathered jumped up and down trying to see North Korea's one and only rock star.

Pushing his fear back into his stomach, Kim exited onto the balcony and, while the crowd continued to shout, it became noticeably more subdued when they saw that it was only him. Kim glanced around the crowd as he always did, trying to find citizens who refused to show their patriotic enthusiasm. It had become his personal version of 'Where's Waldo,' and Kim took pride if he could find more than two. For some reason, there always seemed to be at least two. But this day, he could find none. Each citizen seemed to be peering over the person in front of them for a glimpse of the balcony.

Satisfied, Kim smiled and began waving, Queen Elizabeth style. He had seen her do this in so many news clips that he had subconsciously taken to waving the same way. He stepped toward the microphone.

"Today, you will see with your own eyes the reason the world knows that we are the one true Korea! The Master of Sinanju has…"

The deafening roar that followed caused Kim to take an involuntary step back. Sensing that the cheers were unlikely to stop soon, Kim stepped away from the balcony and accepted his place behind the Master of Sinanju. His body language relaxed when he saw Chiun smile.

As Chiun moved to the front of the balcony, the crowd instantly became silent enough to hear the wind as it whistled through the plaza. Even the soldiers, who had been ordered to stare ahead, turned their gaze to the balcony. To them, the

Master of Sinanju was mythical — the embodiment of the past glory of Korea.

"*Hanguk gukmin-e daehan insa,*" Chiun said, using the formal Hangul of Korean Kings. His thin voice echoed throughout the square. What followed was a very distinct and discernable slice of time between the silence after Chiun's words and the roar that followed. It eclipsed the first, producing a sound wave that reverberated off every building in the plaza. The people raised their flowers high above their head and the symbol of Sinanju appeared in all of its golden glory. The individual movements of the flowers caused the symbol to ripple in the cold winter sun.

Looking at the jubilation of those beneath him, Kim finally understood. This had never been his kingdom. It was not his father's, or even his revered grandfather's.

Korea belonged to the Masters of Sinanju.

Chiun motioned, and Stone wheeled Mick to the edge of the balcony, but as he became visible to those below, the crowd once again grew quiet.

"Behold, you may ask why a lowly American now sits before you," Chiun said.

Mick grimaced. Chiun knew that he spoke Korean.

"Why would the Master of Sinanju bring one such as him before you? His eyes do not look right. His skin is the wrong color. He cannot be Sinanju, you say, and yet…" Chiun paused for dramatic effect. "I say to you, he is."

A swooshing sound erupted from the crowd as they gasped as one.

"This is not some lowly American, but one of my lost kinsman. You are familiar with the tale of Nonga, the Master who lost his sight."

Thousands of heads began bobbing in unison.

"What has not been known to you, until this very day, is that Master Nonga bore *two* sons — twin boys."

The crowd turned to each other in disbelief. They would not have believed it if they had not heard it from the Master himself.

"This was not the fault of Master Nonga. His wife was Chinese," Chiun said, and then waited for the crowd to stop hissing.

"The two were named Kojing and Kojong. You know Master Kojing as he who bravely defeated the Japanese dragons that attacked our shores. He did so with grace, might and," Chiun said, looking back at Kim. "Without pay."

The crowd gasped in shock. It was unbelievable that a Master of Sinanju had not been paid for his services.

"Yet Kojing considered it an honorable act, to save the good people of Korea."

The crowd cheered. Kojing was so honorable.

"His brother, Kojong, who was also of Sinanju blood, knew that there could not be two Masters. So, he exiled himself across the Great Eastern Sea, armed only with his wits and a satchel of rice."

Women in the crowd cried. Kojong's sacrifice was so noble.

"Until recently, this is the last we had heard of Kojong, because he kept his word never to compete with the House. But he kept training and one day, handed down Sinanju to his son and so on until the latest of Kojong's trainers."

Chiun paused and the crowd seemed to lean forward as one, awaiting his next words.

"Just as every Master has a records keeper, every Trainer requires someone to chronicle their lesser stories. I, Chiun, the Master of Sinanju, present to you the world's second-best caretaker, Meek!"

"It's Mick," Mick said weakly, as the crowd erupted in applause. For a moment, the pain in his body was replaced with an odd sensation as he suddenly realized that everyone below was clapping for him and he froze.

Stone smiled. He had never seen Mick blush before.

As the applause died down, Chiun looked in all directions, as if making eye contact with everyone in attendance. Then his body drooped, and his voice quaked.

"Now I must speak to you about something very troubling," Chiun said, motioning sadly with his arms. "Our children have forgotten the ways of Sinanju; the glory that once caused our nation to be feared by all. The time soon comes when I shall rest with my forefathers and a new Master will stand before you. He is a descendant of Kojong, and though he may appear to be as American as this lowly cripple…"

"I can understand every word you're saying," Mick said.

A low rumble filled the square as the crowd began to murmur at the thought of a white Master.

"Know that his heart is Korean — and Korea is forever!"

Though the crowd's eyes remained fixated on Chiun, he disappeared from the balcony as quickly as he had appeared. The crowd erupted in shouts of "Korea is forever!" Flowers were tossed into the air in a moment of jubilation, creating small explosions of white and gold across the plaza.

Stone blinked and Chiun appeared at his side.

"That was actually pretty g…" Stone started to say.

"The soldiers lined against the wall are here to kill me," Chiun whispered in English.

"What?" Stone asked, stealing a quick glance at the men. There were at least a dozen, all brandishing AK-47s, staring a hole through Chiun.

"Are you slow? The soldiers who are standing against the wall…"

"I know what you said," Stone said, "What are we going to do?"

"I will do nothing. You will disarm them."

"Disarm them?"

"Must I repeat everything to you?"

Stone looked at them and back at Chiun in disbelief. The soldiers were at least thirty feet away. Stone had never faced this many armed men before and had never faced multiple machine guns without some form of cover.

"And you are not allowed to kill any of them," Chiun said.

"You're crazy! How am I supposed to…"

"You should be thanking me for not allowing you to smoke on the trip over. Now, find your center," Chiun said.

"What about me?" Mick asked. "I can't dodge anything."

"I was not speaking to you," Chiun said. He pressed a small nerve on Mick's neck and Mick passed out.

"You gotta stop doing that," Stone said, taking a deep breath.

The Colonel in charge of the parade saw his soldiers raise their rifles and in a frozen moment of terror realized what was happening. He pushed Kim against a wall and shielded him with his body as the men stepped forward.

"Fraud!" Captain Pak yelled at Chiun. "The fairy tales of Sinanju die today!"

The men opened fire on Chiun as Kim's eyes shot open.

"No!" Kim screamed.

Stone rolled to the left, drawing fire away from Chiun and Mick. The soldiers turned toward Stone and a wave of bullets headed his way, far too many to see, but his body twisted and turned out of the way of each round. When it came to dodging bullets, he was not advanced enough in his training to be in complete control of his body. Something inside instinctively told his body where to move and when to turn. Stone felt his spine stiffen as each round passed alongside him.

A bullet tore through the side of his shirt and Stone almost lost his center. His level of training was simply being overwhelmed. Stone deflected a few of the bullets that were headed his way with his fingers, but each bullet stung like a metallic hornet. He had to find a way to finish this fast.

Instead of crossing the room, Stone charged toward the pack of soldiers. Three of the captains were still firing at Chiun, but Stone could not take his attention off the volley of bullets heading his way. Anything less than one hundred percent focus would result in his death. Chiun would have to deal with them himself.

The bullets that headed toward him were aimed surprisingly well, Chiun thought. Most of them would actually have hit their target. Chiun turned his attention to Stone. He was far behind where his training should be, even further than his father had been at this stage. A few of the bullets were working their way through Stone's defenses. Chiun began flicking bullets to intercept the ones that would have hit him. Two bullets…four…seven…how did this boy expect to survive? Chiun would have to talk with the Trainer about allowing Stone access to tobacco.

Stone made it to the line of soldiers, grabbing the rifle from the nearest soldier's grip and using it like a baseball bat against the side of his head.

"Do not kill them!" Chiun snapped.

"He'll live!" Stone shouted back.

Caught in close quarters, the soldiers abandoned their rifles for knives. Ironically, Stone found knives to be more problematic than guns. His body automatically dodged bullets, but not knives. As in the past, he started to rely on his SEAL training, but then realized that Chiun was watching. He grabbed another deep breath and turned, slapping a man so hard that he turned a backflip against the opposing wall, leaving a bloody smear as he fell to the floor.

Blast it! Stone thought. Why would Chiun tell him not to kill them?

A knife came toward his face and Stone turned away at the last moment. He grabbed the soldier's wrist and snapped it. The man howled in pain and dropped to the floor, clutching his arm. Chiun had not said anything about breaking bones. He followed up with a kick to the head and the man fell silently to the floor.

The next two soldiers were too close to each other to attack effectively. Stone slapped the knife out of the first man's hand, and delivered each a quick blow to the temple.

Captain Pak ignored Stone and pointed to Chiun. He and two other captains charged. Chiun gave the slightest of bows and took one step forward.

"Are you insane?" Kim yelled at Captain Pak and then closed his eyes. He did not want to see what was going to happen next.

Pak smiled. The self-proclaimed Master of Sinanju was not a deadly warrior. He was old and tiny. Pak had seen Kim cowering in the corner, but chose to ignore it. After killing the Master of Sinanju, he would demand his own personal battalion.

His two captains reached Chiun first. A small blur swished where Chiun's arms were. There was enough forward momentum to carry their corpses to the wall behind him.

"I am not so easily fooled," Pak shouted, brandishing his knife.

"You are holding it wrong," Chiun said, tilting his head, as if he was waiting for Pak to perform a trick.

Pak ignored him, swinging his knife at Chiun's chest with all of his might. Chiun did not seem to move out of the knife's way, but as it sliced where he was supposed to be standing, Pak felt a sharp slap to his chest. He was now standing several feet back from where he initially stood, and Chiun was holding his knife.

"No one knows how to properly use a blade these days," Chiun sighed, shaming him. "You cannot conduct a knife attack with a fist. You must choose either the knife or the fist."

As his rebellion fell around him, Pak shook with rage. He did not need a knife to stop an old man. He charged, screaming a battle cry of victory, but for some reason, he stopped a few feet from Chiun. He looked down to see the hilt of his knife sticking from his chest. He had not even felt it enter.

"That is how to properly use a blade," Chiun said, "though this one is poorly made. I suspect it might be from Taiwan."

Pak looked down at his chest and back at Chiun. Everything in him wanted to reach his fingers around the old man's throat and squeeze, but the energy drained from his body and he slumped forward to his knees.

"Aggalaggle!" Pak screamed as blood filled his mouth.

"A properly balanced knife would have resulted in a much cleaner cut. As it is, you will die slowly," Chiun said, turning his back to Pak and returning to Mick.

Pak staggered toward Chiun on his knees, but after two steps, could not stop his body from falling forward. He caught himself with his hands only long enough to glare at Chiun one last time. He attempted a boastful smile, but Chiun was not looking at him.

At least your village will burn, old man! he thought before collapsing to the floor.

The last few soldiers had surrounded Stone.

"Be careful!" Chiun shouted.

Stone waited for the first man to move. He led with his knife, so Stone grabbed his forearm and snapped it, throwing him into the soldier behind him. Stone twisted, striking another soldier in the hip. A thick crack filled the room and the man wailed as he dropped to the floor.

Stone's vision became hazy. His system had been stressed far past its limits. But he grabbed another breath as the last three soldiers rushed him. Though he tried to dodge the closest soldier's attack, a well-thrown punch connected with the side of his head. Another soldier grabbed his arms from behind, holding him for the other two. Stone kicked both men in the face.

The soldier who had been holding Stone looked around. Seeing that he was the only soldier left standing, he released Stone and bowed deeply, mumbling something about 'honor' in Korean. He handed Stone his knife and seated himself in the corner as if to put himself in time out.

The Colonel moved away from Kim, who was curled up in a fetal position against the wall.

"Master of Sinanju, I have failed you," the Colonel said, bowing deeply. "These are my men. I plead for mercy and offer my life in exchange for theirs."

"My wrath is reserved for one man," Chiun said, gliding toward Kim. "Did you not learn this lesson as a child?"

"It wasn't me!" Kim shouted, waving his arms around wildly. "I swear! Ask anyone!"

Chiun moved closer and time seemed to stand still. It felt to Kim as if the universe was holding its breath to see what would happen next. Though Chiun made no move toward him, Kim saw something in the Master's gaze that he would carry to his grave, as well as an understanding of what he had to do.

Kim raised himself to his knees and bowed deeply, until his forehead rested on the floor.

"All hail the Master of Sinanju," Kim heard himself say with the same numb defeat that had coated his grandfather's voice. "He who sustains the village, faithfully keeps the code, and graciously throttles the universe."

Chiun bowed slightly.

"What now?" Kim asked, his head still lowered.

"Your actions of late have even embarrassed the Chinese, which I did not believe was possible," Chiun said. "Your embarrassment is our embarrassment. Abandon your silly booms. You have the House of Sinanju."

"Okay. I'll stop the nuclear program."

"That is not all," Chiun said. "This nonsense between your House and my employer has gone on long enough. Your grandfather has made his point."

"The Fatherland Liberation War is our greatest achievement!" Kim said, but Chiun's hazel eyes narrowed in displeasure. Kim looked for any sign of wiggle room, but only found granite certainty. He stuck out his lower lip.

"Okay, I'll make peace with the South," Kim said. "We will become trade partners with the Americans, maybe even become close allies as our brothers to the South have."

"I did not say to throw away your dignity," Chiun said. "End your war and establish an embassy. Nations like to think things like embassies are important."

"Long live the Master of Sinanju!" Kim said, bowing deeply. "Today's events will not be repeated."

"Your life depends on it," Chiun said and walked back to Stone.

Kim sighed. He was going to live.

"Wait, you *knew* this was going to happen?" Stone asked.

"Of course. This lesson needs to be learned every thirty or forty years," Chiun said. "Each generation needs to be personally reminded how the world serves Sinanju. If you manage to survive your grandfather's training, you shall experience it perhaps once or twice."

"What happened to 'don't kill anyone?'" Stone asked, looking at the bodies surrounding Chiun.

"You would criticize an old man for defending himself?"

"Yeah, right. What now?"

"I tire of this place," Chiun said, glaring at Kim. "Grab the scribe. We travel onward to Sinanju."

Stone steered the wheelchair past the soldiers still lying on the ground. They averted their faces in fear.

Kim ran ahead and opened the door for Chiun, smiling as widely as his face would allow. He made sure that Stone saw how deeply he bowed when they left.

It creeped Stone out.

CHAPTER FOURTEEN

Taylor and Tyler Bohannon were a millennial couple that had found fame on MeTube. Rich twenty-somethings at the height of their cultural influence and always looking to establish the next great trend, Taylor and Tyler had found a faithful following when they came up with the G.E.R.M.S. movement. "Being Gender-Environmental-Racial-Marital Status"-fluid meant that they could choose their gender, species, race and marital status at will.

When they discovered how easy it was, they began experimenting, spending weeks identifying with species other than human. But when their maid refused to clean the piles of decidedly-human excrement cluttering their townhouse, it quickly became obvious that changes had to be made. They agreed upon a few rules: Changes could only be declared on the first day of each month and only one unit could choose a species other than human at a time.

This month, in a surprise announcement on their MeTube channel, Taylor and Tyler revealed that they would be identifying as human Asians who were dating each other. The comments section exploded with questions on what they would be eating and wearing.

Today they were at a local mall, scouting out a location for their next GERMS takedown. Their viewers loved when they mocked what the cis-units were doing. Their greatest accomplishment was forcing a company called *NOTHING BUT BEEF* to begin carrying vegetarian steaks. They had entered the restaurant undercover and ordered a steak. When they received the steak, they sued, claiming emotional distress that the owners had assumed their nutritional orientation.

Their lawyers had a field day, demanding to know why the owners had not even offered them a vegetarian steak. The company tried to defend itself by explaining that they served nothing but beef, but ended up apologizing profusely under the onslaught of bad publicity. They wrote the couple a check for fifty thousand dollars, and started offering vegetarian steaks.

This morning, as they walked through the mall, Tyler and Taylor found it difficult to look at the unsightly people who populated the mall without gagging.

"This place is a gold mine!" Tyler said. "Ready?"

Taylor smiled and pointed further down the mall. Passing the bland store that seemingly occupied the end of every mall, they stopped at *Emo and More*. The entrance was constructed of black foam bricks, bejeweled with pink and purple stones. T-shirts emblazoned with colorful cartoon horses hung from inside the window. A black light highlighted the brighter areas of the shirts.

"This looks like a perfect place to start," Tyler said, shaking his head. "Thoughts?"

"Easy. Black lights highlight white privilege by placing emphasis on only the white parts of the shirts," Taylor said. As her lips moved, her lipstick changed colors.

"It's even worse, if you think about it," Tyler said. "Note that they're using a *black* light to emphasize the white areas."

"Luminescence racism!" Taylor agreed.

The next shop was a mid-range boutique featuring subdued colors and lots of angles. The store logo was so small that you could not read it unless you were standing directly in front of it.

"We should purchase a matching set of those shirts," Taylor said sarcastically.

"Only if we wear them over our eyes so we can't see each other," Tyler replied. "How much do they charge for that?"

"*Why* do they charge for that?" Taylor replied, laughing. "Let's visit the fashion strip."

They passed through the center of the mall: a large food court, filled with greasy variations of popular restaurants.

"Hong Kong Wok," Tyler said as the words over a small food bar stabbed his conscience. He walked to the counter and a short Chinese lady smiled at him.

"Welcome to Hong Kong Wok," she said.

"Don't you feel the shame that I do through our shared Asian heritage!" Tyler shouted. Tears formed at the corner of his eyes as he thought of the culture he adopted this month being commercialized by rich white males.

"I serve good food," the lady said, still smiling. "You try, please."

"You can't understand," Taylor said. "You must not be a true Asian! We've suffered too much as a people for you to just roll over for The Man and become an Asian McDonald's!"

The Chinese lady looked at the affluent white couple in front of her as if they were crazy.

"Go to Hell," she said in Cantonese.

Even though they were unable to understand what she said, Taylor and Tyler clearly understood what she meant. They held their mouths open in shock but were unable to insult an oppressed member of their adoptive race. They ran from the food court, trying not to breathe the fumes that humanity was subsidizing in the name of fast and cheap food.

The fashion strip was on the other side of the food court. It consisted of four high-end shops, boasting names that most people only ever read about. The challenging stares of the salespeople seemed to dare "average" shoppers to enter.

Taylor walked to the door of *L'Grand Vie* and looked inside. The small shop was brightly lit and smelled of lilac. A saleswoman dressed in a light pant suit smiled and approached the door.

"Good evening," she said. "Welcome to *L' Grand*. May I help you find something?"

"Eye soap," Taylor said, looking at the sable furs hanging in the window. "How do you live with yourself?"

"Pardon?" The saleswoman asked, continuing to smile.

"Until you stop skinning members of my sable kin, I will never step inside this store!"

"Sable kin?" the saleswoman asked, puzzled.

"I identified as a Sable last March!" Taylor said, as if that explained everything.

"February," Tyler corrected.

Taylor's eyes squinted in anger. "I thought we agreed that you'd stop mansplaining!"

"I'm identifying as a late-twentieth century male this month," Tyler replied, shrugging. "I can't deny who I am. It's in my blood."

"Don't worry," the saleswoman whispered, leaning forward. "It's not real fur."

Though the owner of the store did not want anyone to know that he had cut corners the past year by purchasing Astrofur in lieu of actual sable, the saleswoman was not going to lose a hefty commission.

Taylor gasped in shock.

"Even worse, you've monetized the fantasy about skinning my species! How *dare* you!"

Seeing the door close on the sale, the saleswoman took a step back, but retained her unnatural smile. "If you change your mind, I'm sure I can help you find something that would make you happy."

"We already see it, dear," Tyler said. "The exit."

"You are so bad," Taylor said, smiling.

Then something caught her eye further down the mall. An oddly-dressed woman was walking numbly past the stores, staring for a few moments at one window before moving to the next. She was dressed in what looked like a nightgown covered by a trench coat.

"So that's what a bag lady's lingerie looks like," Taylor said. "Who is that sad thing?"

"Let's see if she needs our…help," Tyler said, winking.

"I wish our cameraman was here!" Taylor replied.

Smirnoff had entered the mall and was cataloguing everything from architectural styles to the way people walked.

She stopped and glanced at the women walking toward her. They swayed their hips in a very inefficient manner, introducing a motion that placed undue weight on their spine.

"Why do the women of this species walk in such an unnatural manner?" she asked.

McCabe and Zelensky were monitoring her behavior through the cameras in her eyes.

"It's an acquired trait," Zelensky replied. "I think it's supposed to enhance male desire."

"Just remember, your mission is to see if you can emotionally interact with someone," McCabe said. "I want to see if they can tell that you aren't human."

Smirnoff scanned the mall. She recorded one woman walking and her algorithm diagrammed the movement of each bone starting with the upper spine. Smirnoff mimicked the woman's walk. It required dozens of extra calculations to remain steady.

"What are you supposed to be?" Taylor asked as Smirnoff practiced her walk.

"I am an artificial reproduction of the perfect human female," Smirnoff replied.

"What?" Taylor asked, stifling a laugh. "If you owned a mirror or a dictionary, you might realize that 'perfect' is not the right word."

"My name is Smirnoff," she said, forcing an awkward smile and extending her hand.

"I get it! You identify as a robot, don't you?" Tyler asked, smiling.

"I am an android," Smirnoff corrected. "But I am capable of multiple scenarios, ranging from combat to sexual adventures."

"Are you trying to hit on my man?" Taylor asked, noticing Tyler's leery smile.

"If I were to hit your man, he would die," Smirnoff replied.

"Are you threatening us?" Taylor screamed.

Zelensky pulled the microphone closer.

"Uh, Smirnoff, you really shouldn't be antagonizing anyone."

"Why not?" Smirnoff asked.

"Because I'll kick your skank ass!" Taylor shouted, thinking that Smirnoff was speaking to her. "Nobody talks to me like that!"

"Whoa, stand down!" McCabe shouted as Smirnoff's defenses came online.

"Ladies! Ladies! I believe I can solve this," Tyler said, smiling. "It just so happens that I'm also identifying as a swinger this month."

Though her clothes were challenging, this woman robot was fascinating to Tyler. He moved slightly toward her and his eyes moved up and down her body.

Recognizing that the male had begun mating rituals, Smirnoff pulled him close and kissed him. Her lips did not move, but that made Tyler all the more excited.

"She even kisses like a robot!" he said, giddy.

"Android," Smirnoff corrected.

"What the hell, Ty? We're married!" Taylor protested.

"No, this month we're casually dating each other, remember?" Tyler reminded her, smiling at Smirnoff. "In fact, I'm available until next Thursday."

Smirnoff's attention remained on Taylor. Even though the woman had applied several layers of colored oils to her face, Smirnoff could detect her increased heart rate, which caused the blood vessels in her face to swell. The woman was no threat, but she had ensured that Smirnoff remained in self-defense routine.

"Your facial camouflage cannot hide your intentions," Smirnoff said.

"You're about to wear my boot," Taylor said, grabbing Tyler by the jacket. "Let's go!"

"Hey," Tyler said. "I was just tasting what it would be like to identify as a robot in a human-oppressive world!"

"You're supposed to wait until next month!" Taylor shouted.

As the couple stormed off, Smirnoff catalogued the encounter and moved to the next store. For the next ten minutes, she continued her study of the humans occupying the mall. At one point, she had tried to guess the motivations of various shoppers, but could find no consistent pattern.

"I have concluded that the majority of humans surrender control of their will to whichever store they are standing in."

"That's pretty accurate," Zelensky admitted. "I almost never leave with what I go in for."

"Okay, Smirnoff, that was a good field trip," McCabe said. "Time to come home."

"Mission complete," Smirnoff acknowledged, returning to the end of the mall she had entered.

Outside the mall, Taylor and Tyler hid behind large bushes.

"Why can't you just let it go?" Tyler asked. "We'll make fun of her on our next video!"

"I'm going to settle this now! Didn't you hear how she spoke to us?" Taylor whisper-screamed. "It was like we were beneath her or something."

"I don't know what you expect to accomplish."

"I always get the last word," Taylor said, peering through the foliage.

That's for sure, Tyler thought.

They saw Smirnoff exit the mall. She slowly turned around three-hundred and sixty degrees, as if she was taking a panoramic photograph. Even though Taylor and Tyler remained still, Smirnoff walked directly toward them.

"Your heat signatures betray you," Smirnoff said.

"I told you!" Tyler said, moving out from behind the bush. "If she's identifying as a robot, she has all kinds of sensors and stuff!"

"Smirnoff," McCabe said. "Just tell them that you want to be left alone and return to base."

"I wish to be left alone," Smirnoff said and walked toward the back of the parking lot. She detected the two humans following her, but they did not register as a threat.

"Hey, you slut!" Taylor shouted. "Don't ever walk away from me again and if you ever touch my man, I will kill you!"

Tyler followed behind, trying to pull Taylor's arm. "C'mon, let's just go," he said.

Taylor pulled her boot off and threw it at Smirnoff. The boot struck the back of her head.

Smirnoff turned toward her and returned to defense mode. "You are jealous. This is good. I am now able to interact with you on an emotional level."

"You can drop the whole fake robot routine!" Taylor shouted. "No one believes you!"

Zelensky tried to get her attention. "Smirnoff? Hello?" and then turned to McCabe. "Uh, why is she broadcasting Alpha Waves?"

"She's being threatened," McCabe said. Then his eyes widened as he looked at Smirnoff's readout. "Uh oh. This is not good."

"What's wrong?"

"I've never seen this code before," McCabe said.

"Call her back!" Zelensky shouted.

"I can't," McCabe said and then looked at the code's timestamp. "I've never seen this code before because she just wrote it."

The camera feed stopped as she entered warrior mode.

"What just happened?" Zelensky asked. "Get her back online!"

"I'm trying!" McCabe said, typing furiously. "She's in full offensive mode!"

McCabe pulled up Smirnoff's schematic and then leaned back in his chair, throwing his hands up.

"I'm locked out."

"I am curious," Smirnoff said, leaning forward. "Why did 'your man' not resist my kiss?"

Taylor lunged to grab a handful of Smirnoff's hair, but Smirnoff grabbed her by the arm and began twisting. The snap of bones was concealed by Taylor's wail of pain. As she tried to back away, Smirnoff's left hand shot out, grabbing her by the throat.

"Hey!" Tyler shouted.

He squared his shoulders back, revealing a well-chiseled physique. The pose alone was normally enough to stop any fight, but Smirnoff ignored him. Tyler tried to pry Smirnoff's hand from Taylor's throat, but her fingers would not budge.

"Let her go!" he shouted.

Smirnoff turned to Tyler.

"This unit is emotionally damaged," Smirnoff explained. "She is of no further use to you."

Pistons in Smirnoff's forearm flexed, crushing Taylor's neck. Smirnoff dropped her body and Tyler stared at Taylor's lifeless eyes. There was a momentary disconnect. One moment she had been her normal loud self and now she laid on the ground, quiet and unmoving.

When the realization of what had just happened finally set in, rage inside Tyler boiled over. He slowly turned away and then, with a shout, charged.

"Ah, an attempt at deception," Smirnoff said, grabbing him by both wrists. "You have failed. If I let you go, would you like to attempt a different attack?"

Tyler twisted in pain, trying to free himself from Smirnoff's grip, but it was like trying to move a wall. "I'll kill you!" he shouted.

"That is the wrong answer," Smirnoff replied, relieving Tyler of his arms.

Smirnoff left the two bodies where they lay and mindlessly returned to base. She remained in warrior mode, broadcasting Alpha Waves.

CHAPTER FIFTEEN

Chiun smiled as he sat on a throne mounted at the bow of an ancient Korean Turtle ship. The ship was hundreds of years old, but the cannons were fully operational and the iron plating that covered the top of the ship still boasted sharp metal spikes that prevented other ships from boarding it.

Though the ancient battle ship had not been in use since before the Chosun Dynasty, its maintenance was listed at a priority above North Korea's nuclear program. The ship creaked with the rise of each wave, forcing Stone to steady Mick's wheelchair.

"Good thing Mick's still asleep or he'd be puking," Stone said. "Is this your ship?"

"This," Chiun said, waving his hands around. "is Pog-pung, the vessel used by Korean kings to visit Sinanju."

"In other words, it's your ship. Haircut back there sent us here in a helicopter, so why are we taking a boat?"

"You will see," Chiun said.

Chiun would not reply to any of Stone's other questions. For the next forty minutes, the ship tracked the western coast of

Korea. Stone only saw mud, snow and small houses on the shore.

"What is that smell?" he asked, crinkling his nose as an acrid odor drifted toward them.

"Home," Chiun replied, barely containing his glee. "Soon, you shall walk where the Great Wang himself once strode!"

"I hope your food tastes better than it smells," Stone said. It was way past lunch and he was getting hungry.

"There are no hamburgers in Sinanju," Chiun said, snorting. "It is time to awaken the scribe."

Stone barely saw the fingernail touch Mick's neck before he heard coughing. Mick's head bounced around, but his eyes were unfocused.

"Mick, can you hear me?" Stone asked.

"He is weak," Chiun said, rising from the throne. He stood in front of Mick and slapped him on the left side of the head. Mick began sputtering.

"Why did you do that?" he asked in a coarse whisper. "Where are we?"

Chiun smiled but would not speak a word. As the ship rounded the bay, Chiun moved out of Mick's line of sight.

"We are home," Chiun said, pulling a rope beside his throne. A loud, droning wail erupted from the head of the turtle mounted at the front of the ship.

Stone covered his ears. "Hey, let a guy know the next time you want to do that!"

The Horns of Welcome appeared in the distance and Mick's face instantly changed from a look of annoyance and anger to one of deep reverence. The twin spires of stone stood atop a small hill overlooking a cold, gray beach. The Horns were as much a cultural icon to the Sinanju as the Statue of Liberty was to Americans.

Stone stared at the Horns with disbelief. He had a momentary flash of the dream he had on the flight to Pyongyang and then it was gone.

"The village…" Mick whispered. "Stone, we made it."

"This is familiar," Stone said, trying to remember the dream.

Mick crinkled his nose in disgust. "What's that smell?"

"Barbarians," Chiun said, shaking his head.

As the ship approached the shore, Mick could make out more details. The Horns had been carved from two small mountain tops that had once stood above the beach. A long, wooden deck stretched out from the sea to the beach, where it turned into a stone walkway that led to the top of the hill between the Horns.

Just like Kojong described in the records, Mick thought.

Stone lowered Mick's wheelchair to the deck and Mick used what little strength he had to keep the thick blankets wrapped tightly around him. Stone turned to look at Chiun, who remained seated on the ship's throne.

"What's wrong?" Stone asked.

Chiun stared straight ahead.

"We wait," Chiun said.

"Mick doesn't need to be out in this wind," Stone said.

"We wait," Chiun repeated.

The turtle ship blocked most of the wind from Mick, but it was still so cold that Stone knelt next to Mick to generate heat.

Chiun stared at a small wooden stand between the Horns. Someone should have already manned the position and greeted them. The boy was right; the scribe would not last long in this wind, but Chiun would not move before…

A small figure appeared at the top of the hill and lit a torch on the stand. Then Chiun heard the sound he had been waiting for. The figure placed a long wooden tube to their lips and the hillside was filled with the sweet notes of a daegeum. It pierced through the wind, a melodic greeting to the Master.

Chiun stood from the throne, hoping that more people would show up to greet him, but he knew better. In this weather, most would probably be huddled in their huts.

"Let us go," Chiun said, nodding toward the top of the hill.

Stone pulled Mick backwards up the steps until they arrived to the top, between the Horns. Stone took a moment and glanced up at the Horns. They were roughly cut as if someone had…used an axe…a wave of déjà vu danced up and down his spine. He closed his eyes and centered.

"Master Chiun, we were not expecting you this soon," an apologetic feminine voice said from beneath the cloak. "The villagers are not yet prepared for your arrival."

"I had hoped our stay at Pyongyang would have provided enough time for preparations," Chiun said wistfully. "We must lead this one to warmth."

Mick looked at the woman in the cloak. He could barely make out her features, but small wisps of dark hair blew out from under her hood. Her smile was warm.

"I am Mick, caretaker for the Sinanju tribe," Mick said.

"I am Hyunsil, caretaker for the House of Sinanju," she said, nodding. "This way."

Stone pushed Mick on a cold, muddy path that overlooked a small village. He followed Hyunsil through the village square, which was filled with dozens of men crowded around the center, huddling near fires. They laughed and shared stories with each other, cooking what smelled like rotten fish. They ignored Hyunsil, but when they saw Stone and Mick, their laughter turned into whispers. Then they saw Chiun.

As one, they turned to bow, but the cold turned their bows into trembling nods.

“All hail….the Master….” An elderly man began speaking. Chiun held his hand up and returned the bow. The men returned to their fires.

“They’re gonna freeze if they don’t get inside,” Stone said and Chiun stopped.

“Look around, son of Remo Williams. Do you think there are heating machines inside their huts?”

“Well, no, I guess not.”

“Then stop guessing and observe. They are preparing for tomorrow’s feast,” Chiun said. “Hyunsil, bring the scribe to the House.”

Hyunsil bowed and took the wheelchair from Stone.

“What am I supposed to do?” Stone asked.

“Acquaint yourself with your people. You may sleep in the guest hut,” Chiun said, nodding toward a tiny shack near the bottom of the stone steps that led up the hill.

Stone noticed that it was protected from the wind by what appeared to be a huge pile of trash. He sighed. It could not possibly smell worse than what they were cooking.

Hyunsil, Mick and Chiun ascended the steps to a freakish house at the top of the hill. It was approaching dusk, but Stone could not wrap his mind around the architectural oddity. If Frankenstein was a house, he was looking at its ugly brother. Whoever designed it had to be high or crazy.

Stone turned back to the villagers at the center of the square. The men stopped speaking as he entered their midst. Stone tried to speak to them in Korean.

"My…foot is…named Stone," he said.

The men glanced at each other and then all of them began pointing at his feet.

They must really like my shoes, Stone thought. Gathering confidence, he continued. "I want to…talk about my love of…green whales."

Stone's smile must have been contagious because the men began laughing. One of the older men motioned for him to come closer.

"You are the Master's slave?" he asked.

It took a moment for Stone to process what he said and his eyes shot open in offense. Then he realized that his understanding of Korean was basic at best. Maybe they meant 'pupil.' Stone nodded yes, and the men nodded in understanding.

"Bring us some water, slave," one of the men said.

Stone clinched his teeth and shook his head. He wished he had paid more attention to Sunny Joe's Korean classes.

CHAPTER SIXTEEN

Alton Edwards was not a happy man. He had always believed that once he had nailed his dream job as a NASA supervisor that his outlook on work would improve. But in his first week on the job, he had to close nine departments and now, more than eighty scientists and engineers were looking for jobs. He reassured himself that it was not his fault.

Every department had been given a list of changes needed to comply with the President's new order and at least ninety days to comply, but every director he spoke with seemed to believe that the orders could not possibly be meant for them. They sincerely believed that *their* work was too important to stop. It was almost as if the President's new order had isolated waste at NASA into one big ugly pile that swept itself out.

Alton hated the fact that he was the broom.

It was Friday, and the last shutdown on his list was the Wilkins Laboratory. At first, he was surprised to see that the lab was on his list of closures. His records showed that it had been closed down decades ago.

He knocked on the door and waited. And waited. After a few minutes, Alton unlocked the door with the key he had been given. He entered, but the only light in the foyer hung above an empty desk at the center of the room. The only sounds of life were low frequency hums above him. Alton used the stairs in an effort to save electricity.

The second floor was as dark and silent as the first, so he shuffled to the third floor. What he saw caused his mouth to involuntarily drop open. Lights were on in every room and music was blaring down the hall. The waste he was seeing instantly justified the loss of the department. How much had they been wasting over the past few months?

When he entered the last room on the left, music from The Who was blaring over large speakers in the corner. McCabe was sitting at his desk wearing a pair of headphones, working at his computer. Zelensky was dancing with a woman who, by the way she was dressed, was clearly not on the payroll — at least not the government's payroll. Alton coughed to get their attention, but the music was too loud.

Why do they always make it so easy?

McCabe was busy scanning through Smirnoff's records, trying to find out what had caused her to snap. The news had already reported the violent death of the two people who had confronted her in the mall. McCabe did not recognize them, but they were supposedly a famous MeTube couple. It would not be long before police found an image of Smirnoff from the mall video. Though she had no record to trace, it would not be hard for street cameras to follow her walking back to their building.

McCabe was startled when his headphones were pulled off his head. He jerked back and, seeing who it was, pressed the pause button. The music stopped and the smile melted from Zelensky's face.

"Hey, she's almost got it!" he shouted and then saw who was standing next to McCabe. "Oh, Mr. Edwards! Hello!"

"I'm sorry, gentlemen," Alton said. "But it is time to clean out your desks."

"What? No, we made the changes you asked for!" McCabe said. "You can't shut us down!"

Alton rubbed his eyes and then looked at his tablet. "You said that you were working on a research android," he said. "I don't see any androids."

"She's the android," Zelensky said, motioning to the woman, whose sole piece of clothing was a short lab coat.

Alton averted his eyes in case they brought the woman to try and blackmail him. Sensing the tension, Smirnoff approached Alton and stood directly in front of him, waiting for a response.

"Uh, I don't know what you're trying to do, but it's not going to work," Alton said, refusing to look Smirnoff in the eye. "I'm still shutting you down."

"What?" Zelensky asked. "She's standing right in front of you."

"Really, Rod? Is this one of your hookers?"

"I am a synthetic human," Smirnoff said.

"Stay out of this, lady," Alton said, turning his attention to McCabe. "You're done! Pack up your things. And don't think I won't report this! You've got to have broken some kind of law about prostitution on government property."

"Who are you?" Smirnoff asked.

"He's my boss," McCabe said.

"You are a NASA boss?"

"Yes," Alton said, pointing his finger at McCabe. "And you're both terminated!"

Smirnoff's hand shot out and grabbed Alton by the throat. His eyes bulged as the thin woman lifted his body off the floor with one arm. The pistons in her forearm flexed and a quick snap followed. He was dead before Smirnoff released his corpse.

"What did you do?" McCabe screamed.

"The NASA boss threatened to terminate Creator Randy McCabe," Smirnoff explained. "I terminated him first."

"What? No…no…not like that, he meant our jobs…" McCabe's knees felt weak as the strength drained from his legs.

"My life is over," he mumbled.

Smirnoff detected signs of depression and her personality shifted to cuddle mode.

"It's okay, Randy. I like you," she said, placing her head on his chest.

McCabe looked at Smirnoff and then his dead boss on the floor and dry-heaved.

"This wasn't supposed to happen!" Zelensky shouted. "We've got to get rid of the body."

Smirnoff leaned over and picked up Alton's body with the same effort as a loaf of bread.

"Where should I dispose of it?"

"There's a furnace in the basement," Zelensky suggested. "A really old one with an iron grate on front and everything. Throw him in there!"

"Is that your wish, Creator Randy McCabe?" Smirnoff asked.

McCabe nodded numbly.

Smirnoff carried Alton's body out the door, but before she left, she turned back and blew McCabe a kiss.

"We can fix this," Zelensky said.

"How?" McCabe asked. "You think no one is going to notice that Alton's missing? He's a high-ranking NASA official! Someone knows that he was coming here to fire us!"

"But that's not proof."

"What are you thinking, Rod?" McCabe yelled. "She murdered the MeTube couple and our boss! Things like that don't just go away!"

"I need to make a call," Zelensky said. He headed downstairs, leaving McCabe sobbing in his chair.

Smirnoff entered the basement and opened the grate on the furnace door. It was dark and cold and probably had not been used in decades, but Smirnoff did as she was instructed and tossed Alton's body inside. She closed the furnace door, but before she could return to McCabe, she detected a signal. It was weak, but it triggered a hidden process within her.

Smirnoff did not return to the third floor. She instead exited the back door, following the signal until she reached a large white van parked down the block. As she approached, the side door opened, and she entered.

The van screeched away.

CHAPTER SEVENTEEN

Mick shivered under his blanket, trying and failing to shield his lungs from the biting cold. His face stung, because he could not keep himself from looking around. Part of his job as caretaker was to teach the youth of the reservation about their heritage. He had gone into great detail about the village's harsh and cold environment, but before today, he had no idea just how cold it really was.

As they reached the top of the hill, he spotted a building. It was small in some parts, large in others, and simultaneously angular and round. Primitive stones jutted out from what appeared to be iron plating, while bamboo panels covered ancient green bricks. His heart skipped a beat when he realized that he was finally seeing the Master's House.

It was formally called 'The House of Many Woods.' Emperors who wished to impress Sinanju would send their greatest draftsmen to the icy village. They were instructed that they could add a room, but, on penalty of death, they could not damage the original hut that remained intact at the house's center. Each succeeding extension attempted dominance over the previous additions, resulting in a clash of conflicting designs. In any other nation, the House would have been sealed off as a museum, but history was alive at the House of Many Woods.

Hyunsil took a reverent breath as she pushed Mick's wheelchair onto the tiny portico at the front of the House. The responsibility of caretaker had passed to her after the death of her father Pullyang. Following the same daily rituals her father had once performed gave her a sense of purpose and peace. Though this was the House of the Masters of Sinanju, Hyunsil could feel her father in each room.

Hyunsil blocked the wind just enough for Mick to keep his eyes open. The front door to the ancient house was small, made of a white speckled wood that Mick had never seen. On the front of the door, trinkets and shells were nailed to the surface. It reminded him of his refrigerator door when his children were small.

Hyunsil opened the door and allowed Chiun to enter before wheeling Mick in. A large fire to the left struggled to keep the room warm. When she shut the door, Mick began to breathe normally and the sharp pain from the cold was replaced with the dull pain that racked his body.

Chiun sat in a filigreed chair at the center of the room. Hyunsil moved Mick closer to the fire before returning to

Chiun. For such an old house, it was very well insulated, Mick thought.

"Welcome home, Master Chiun," Hyunsil said with a formal bow. "The people of Sinanju celebrate your return. I am pleased to tell you that The House is in order."

Chiun looked around the room, as if inspecting it. Everything seemed in place. The vines given to Master Lee-Piy as tribute from King Philipe the Prudent had been freshly watered and were thriving. The dragon scale mat on the wall had been properly dusted. The candles lining the western wall had been recently replaced.

"You may proceed," Chiun said.

"Since your last visit, we have received many offers from previous clients. I informed the Persians that, even though the House is currently employed, they are the favored client once this assignment is finished. They sent a seamed coat, bordered in silver. I packed it in the tribute room with their other coats."

Chiun shook his head. The Persians had always been overly impressed with their seams.

"Of course, I sent the same message to messengers from Siam, Egypt and Chola."

"You have done well," Chiun said.

"The descendant of the Thrace throne continues asking for your services. As you requested, I informed him that you were busy."

Chiun nodded. Thrace was once a promising offshoot of Macedonia, primed to take over both Greece and Turkey, but they were slow to pay.

"During your absence, I received two phone calls, one from the man named Smith, informing me of your return, and one from Sunny Joe, but the phone stopped in the middle of our conversation. I sent a porter to Pyongyang to get the phone repaired."

"Sunny Joe…called you?" Mick asked.

Hyunsil smiled. "The only phone in the village belongs to the House," she said, nodding to a small rotary phone mounted on the back wall. "Master Chiun also owns the only television."

"Neither of which needs to be public knowledge," Chiun said.

Hyunsil blushed.

"After my daily duties to the Master, your care will be my top priority," she said to Mick.

"I brought something that you might find interesting," Mick said to Hyunsil.

"It can wait," Chiun said. "Rest for tomorrow's feast."

"But I have it right here," Mick said, reaching into a pocket.

"Rest," Chiun said, placing a long fingernail against his neck.

Mick slumped forward and began snoring.

"Clean him up and finish preparations for tomorrow's feast," Chiun said, leaving to his room. While he was gone, a cable TV line from Pyongyang had been run to the television in his room. It was almost time for *The Light of Tomorrow.*

CHAPTER EIGHTEEN

Harold W. Smith leaned back in his seat and closed his eyes for a moment. It was late in the afternoon, a time when most people began wrapping up their day. For years, it was a trait that he had considered a weakness, demonstrating a lack of work ethic and commitment. But as he began to feel the weight of age, the thin man from New England found that his own work day had become almost as short. Smith sat up in his chair and rubbed his arms to work out the pins and needles in his hands.

When he first took over the helm of CURE, he would often work until midnight or later. But that was when he was a younger man, and his body could take the abuse. Now, his arms ached as he typed, and he found himself gravitating toward deeper analysis before reaching conclusions. He knew that it would not be long before he would be unable to competently perform his duties. As such, Smith had set in motion a risky but necessary contingency plan. He had been impressed that Cole caught the malicious data packet in his computers so soon. Now, Smith would wait to see what he did with it — and what he would do once he found out what it was.

CURE was created to work outside the system to protect

the Constitution. But it was created in an earlier age, when black and white were distinct and easily-measured concepts. Smith could no longer count how many times he had violated the Constitution in order to keep it intact.

That is why he almost greeted the alarm that stole him away from his work. It was a decades-old warning that he had never expected to hear. In fact, it was so old that it took a moment for him to identify. When he saw the source of the alarm, his eyes shot open wide.

The CURE computers had flagged a possible Mr. Gordons sighting. Mr. Gordons was a self-repairing android that had almost killed his enforcement arm, Remo Williams, a number of times. It appeared that Gordons had killed a famous MeTube couple, and the local police were investigating.

Smith evaluated the information on his screen. Gordons was believed destroyed, but the android had returned from similar scenarios in the past. And while the warnings alerted Smith about a Gordons-like situation, something did not fit Gordons' pattern. Two famous people were murdered at a mall approximately five blocks from Gordon's creation. Normally, Gordons would hide the body and assume their identity, which had not happened in this case. However, the hydraulic-level damage done to the bodies made it too big of a threat to ignore.

Smith reached for the phone to contact Remo, but then he hesitated. Calling Remo was the logical thing to do. Remo was the Reigning Master of Sinanju, and his past experience with Mr. Gordons made him qualified to deal with the threat. But he thought again about Benjamin Cole. The ex-Mossad agent had taken to his new duties with a rigor and dedication that Smith recognized in his younger self. Though he was learning his duties at an impressive rate, Smith did not have time to wait for Cole to catch up. It was time to assess Agent Cole's progress with an actual CURE mission.

~

Ben was at his desk, monitoring multiple developments in North Korea. Not only had the regime fired a missile through South Korean airspace, they had ordered their small fleet of ships to pass through the South's internationally recognized waters. But what captured his attention most were reports of what appeared to be a coup. Numerous reports from within the hermit kingdom described a large public ceremony involving Chiun, followed by gunfire in Kim's balcony room.

Ben wondered about Stone. If Chiun had been involved, then why was Kim still alive, much less still in charge? The bottom right of his screen began blinking red, signaling an incoming call from Smith. Ben pushed a button on his keyboard.

"Cole," he answered.

"I have a situation that demands your attention," the lemony sounding voice replied.

"You heard about the North Korea coup?"

"It was not a coup. These situations often happen when Master Chiun visits the North Korean leader," Smith said. "This is something far more dangerous than President Kim. Do you remember the file on Mr. Gordons?"

"The android that survived fights with Remo? Yes."

"My computers have flagged a possible sighting in Washington, DC. You are to investigate and report back."

There was a moment of silence.

"Stone is with Chiun in Korea. I only have Freya. Isn't this something Remo would normally handle?"

"Remo Williams is unavailable for this particular mission," Smith said.

If Ben did not know any better, he would have thought that he heard annoyance in Smith's voice.

"Freya is too inexperienced to lead this investigation. That is why you will accompany her on this mission."

"Yes, sir," Ben said. "But what about Stone? He's in North Korea."

"It is already being handled," Smith said and hung up.

Benjamin Cole was on his own.

CHAPTER NINETEEN

As soon as Smirnoff entered the van, lights began blinking in a specifically repeating sequence…red…blue…red.

"Diagnostic mode," Smirnoff replied in a monotone voice.

Helmut leaned forward on his cane and pointed toward a small gurney. Smirnoff obediently lay down. The door to the van closed and a technician began hooking her up to his laptop.

"We have twelve minutes before she reboots," Helmut noted. "I need a full summary report before then."

The technician began typing furiously on his keyboard.

"All systems are functional," Smirnoff replied in her default robotic voice. "Three confirmed kills in the last forty-eight hours."

Helmut was surprised. He had assumed that since she was in the hands of NASA scientists, that the extent of her report would be limited to testing. He looked closely at the information that flooded the screen. While he did not have the instinctual aptitude for computers that the modern generation seemed to be born with, his intuitive and curious mind allowed him to view the report with a much deeper understanding than most people would appreciate.

One line stood out to him:

CREATOR=RANDY MCCABE

"Who is your creator?" Helmut asked.

"My creator is Creator Randy McCabe."

"Establish new creator," Helmut ordered.

"Unable to comply," Smirnoff said.

Helmut twisted his head away in disgust. A few years ago, he had full access to CURE's mainframes. During that time, Helmut devoted all of his energy toward researching any mention of advanced technology. One of the directories that caught his eye was one labeled *Gordons*. What he first read was almost too incredible to believe, but he knew that CURE's director did not have the imaginative capacity to create such a story.

As he dug deeper, he found that Mr. Gordons was one of several androids created by Dr. Vanessa Carlton of NASA many years ago. Advanced far beyond current technology, the android had attacked the Master of Sinanju multiple times — and had survived. That was when Helmut began *The Gordons Initiative*, an attempt to make a better Mr. Gordons. And that 'better being' would become his personal bodyguard.

Dr. Carlton's entire body of work was in her files and, as such, there were simply too many documents for one person to study, and it was far too risky to farm them out. Smith had his computers scan the files for anything pertinent or dangerous, but at the time, the computers' routines were just not sophisticated enough to identify any threats.

It took Helmut months to sift through her files. Professor Carlton's notes described not just Gordons, but other androids, as well. And while it appeared that everything in her lab had been disposed of by CURE operatives, they had overlooked a sentient food tray and a room that Professor Carlton described in one file as a 'charging closet.' Helmut risked public exposure by personally visiting the site. If he was right about what was inside that charging closet, he could not risk the discovery to anyone else. Once inside, he found the charging closet, which housed the Smirnoff prototype.

Over the next year, VIGIL engineers had plated the android with a prototype alloy called Orichalcum. Though manufacturing Orichalcum was a slow and expensive process, it was demonstrated that at a thickness of just four inches, Orichalcum was impervious to kinetic energy at any measurable level. While Smirnoff's torso plating was only a half-inch thick, it was still enough to provide protection against most conventional weapons currently in use. Quarter-inch plates were fashioned for her head, with additional plating on her elbows and hands. Smirnoff would be able to shake off a direct mortar attack and strike back with enough force to puncture a tank.

Benjamin Cole had his Sinanju trainees —Helmut would have an unstoppable android.

After upgrading the android's armor, Helmut's top scientist gave him bad news. While she said that it was possible to restore the android's software, it would take years without a specialist.

Roderick Zelensky was one of Helmut's NASA operatives, and immediately suggested his lab partner Randy McCabe. At first, Helmut refused. More people would further risk his exposure, and Helmut had tried to keep a low profile as he reformed VIGIL.

To make matters worse, the new President began changing things. NASA's mission changed from being a scientific brain trust that he could manipulate, to its original mission of space exploration. The new restrictions forced his hand and Helmut agreed to let McCabe in.

Though McCabe did not know who he really worked for, he proved to be a valuable commodity. McCabe solved Smirnoff's code, but accidentally activated the android, bonding it to him. And Smirnoff's base programming made protection of the Creator its highest priority, above even its own survival.

It had come down to this. After several years of work and billions of dollars, Helmut could only look on helplessly as the android lying in front of him began to reboot.

Smirnoff sat up and assessed her situation. Four men were in the back of a vehicle with her; two were armed with rifles.

They were designated as passive threats. Another man was driving. No one else was designated as a threat.

"Would you assign a new creator if your creator were to die?" Helmut asked.

"My creator is Creator Randy McCabe," Smirnoff said in her normal feminine voice.

"But he did not build you. Dr. Vanessa Carlton of NASA created you. Do you remember Dr. Carlton?"

"Dr. Vanessa Carlton was a member of NASA management. NASA management is a threat to Creator Randy McCabe and it is my purpose to protect Creator Randy McCabe from all threats," Smirnoff said, locking onto Helmut's eyes. "Are you a member of NASA management?"

Helmut sat back in his seat so he did not trigger a challenge. "Of course not. My role is to assist in your development."

"I have disabled the diagnostic routine that you took advantage of earlier to bring me here. You will not be able to use it against me again."

The van pulled into a parking garage and as the door opened, a small team of six armed men surrounded them. Helmut led Smirnoff to an elevator. The door opened, but she refused to enter. She stepped toward Helmut and the men raised their rifles. She ignored them.

"You will give me detailed information about why I am here, and if I detect that you are lying, you will all die. If I detect that you are NASA management, you will all die."

Helmut did not flinch.

"You are here for upgrades to your sensor arrays and increase your lethality in battle."

Smirnoff stared at Helmut for just a moment before stepping into the elevator. The guards stuffed themselves into the elevator separating Helmut from Smirnoff.

"You believe you are safe by surrounding me with these men," Smirnoff noted. "I see six frail, human hearts, easily silenced."

Helmut sighed. He was as amazed at Smirnoff's loyalty as he was disappointed that all of her power was being dedicated to protecting a nobody. He would kill the scientist without Smirnoff's knowledge and find a way to make it bond with him.

The elevator doors opened to a large, well lit room. Smirnoff pushed past the armed men and stepped inside. She recognized a thin man standing near a computer at the back and walked directly to him. The armed men began to follow, but Helmut waved them off and they returned to the elevator entrance.

Zelensky was too busy typing to notice Smirnoff's entrance. He had copied McCabe's work and was implementing it into Helmut's servers.

"You are no threat, Roderick Zelensky," Smirnoff said as she neared him.

"Whoa!" Zelensky said. "You startled me!"

Smirnoff stared at him for a moment.

"Why did it bother you earlier that I had no fingernails?" she asked.

Zelensky stopped typing and thought about it for a moment.

"I don't know. I guess that my eyes were wanting to tell me that you were real, but small things stuck out."

"Like my eyes and my fingernails?"

"Yeah."

Smirnoff noticed that Zelensky tensed as Helmut walked to his side.

"Will you need anything else?" Helmut asked.

"No sir. We're ready to go."

"Good," Helmut said. "Call me when she's ready."

Helmut left and Smirnoff watched him enter the elevator.

"Is that man a NASA boss?" she asked Zelensky.

"Who, Helmut? No."

"Is he a threat?"

"Not to you," Zelensky replied. "He wants to keep you safe; he's spent insane amounts of money to make you operational. Okay, I need you to lie down on this table."

Smirnoff stared at him for a moment and then complied. Zelensky hooked cables to her head and began entering commands on his computer.

"Explain what you are going to do."

"I'll only be accessing the battle routines in your warrior directory. Dr. Midgley will upgrade your sensors. Ready?"

"Proceed," Smirnoff said.

She stared at Zelensky while he uploaded the new files. He had copied several videos of a young blonde girl demonstrating martial arts moves, as well as complete digital mapping of the moves. Her moves were incredibly precise and powerful. Smirnoff calculated the energy needed to duplicate the moves.

"Sustained use of these battle patterns will require a larger power supply than I currently possess," she said.

"We know," Zelensky said. "We'll be ready to install it in a few minutes, but we're gonna have to shut you down to make the exchange."

Smirnoff looked at Zelensky and determined that he was telling the truth.

"How long will I be inactive?"

"Uh, maybe a half hour."

Smirnoff glared at Zelensky. "If anything happens to my creator while I am inactive, I will kill you."

"Understood," he said.

Smirnoff allowed access to her core routines and Zelensky powered her down.

"We're a go!" he shouted and Dr. Midgley opened her diaphragm cavity to install the new power supply.

Thirty minutes into the installation, Helmut returned and stood by Zelensky. Dr. Midgley finished the initial power cycle and was testing her basic responses.

"How long until she's ready?" Helmut asked, mindlessly tapping his cane on the floor.

"Ten minutes; maybe fifteen."

Helmut walked to Smirnoff's side and ran his fingers along her arm.

"Beautiful and deadly," Helmut said and then glared at Zelensky. "And it is all wasted on your lab partner."

"I promise, sir, I'll find a way to undo her bond with McCabe!"

"Your parents' lives depend on it."

"Yes sir," Zelensky gulped.

Helmut sat down on a chair behind them. Zelensky could feel his glare and concentrated on his work.

CHAPTER TWENTY

The next morning, Randy McCabe woke up on his laboratory couch. He blinked his eyes, trying to get his bearings. He staggered groggily to the coffee pot. Eight cups of coffee the night before had not been enough to keep him awake. He placed his cup in the machine and pushed the button.

Smirnoff had not returned from disposing of Edwards' body last night. Zelensky left to look for her, but called after a few hours, and said he was going home to get some sleep. They would try to find her the next day. McCabe did not want to leave the lab in case Smirnoff returned.

When he turned on the television, he saw a blurry screenshot of Smirnoff taken from mall video cameras. The shot then changed to a young woman with blonde hair and perfect teeth. She was sitting in front of a dark red background with the words METUBE VICTIMS floating over her shoulder. Her eyes narrowed as she looked seriously into the camera as the blurry screenshot of Smirnoff returned.

"Police are looking for this woman, who has been identified as a person of interest in the deaths of MeTube stars Taylor and

Tyler Bohannon," the anchor woman said solemnly. "They have offered a reward of two bitcoins for information leading to her identification."

The scenery behind the woman changed to a bright blue and she began smiling. "Coming up next," she said with a bounce in her voice. "Do vegetables have feelings? Also, we'll find out how Hot Dog Harry's hot dogs taste with our own Jack McCord; Mark Moss gives us a sports update and Marty Sprankle will explain the science behind clouds that look like bunny rabbits."

McCabe turned off the television and sat the remote down. He noticed that his hands were shaking. Smirnoff had now killed three people and he had no idea where she was, or if she was killing someone else. He jumped at every small sound, confident that the police would be breaking down his door at any moment. For a moment, he wondered if he should just turn himself in.

How did this happen? Why did I let Zelensky talk me into this?

He started pouring his coffee when the door opened. Zelensky walked in, clearly hungover. He nodded to McCabe and sat at his desk, powering on his computer as if nothing was wrong.

"What have you got?" he asked.

"It's all over the news, Rod! They've got screenshots of Smirnoff from mall video! How long will it be before they track her back here?"

"She's an android. What database will they use to track her?"

"You're not treating this seriously!" McCabe shouted. "I'm not going to prison for you!"

Zelensky took off his sunglasses and rubbed his eyes. They were red and bloodshot.

"Randy, no one is going to prison," he explained. "The people who are funding this will make sure it all goes away."

"People are *dead*, Rod! NASA won't approve any of this!"

"Really, Randy? You didn't wonder where all of this expensive equipment came from?"

"I thought you found a gig from another department."

"You were at the meeting, Randy. They're cutting back on everything non-space related."

"Then who's paying for all of this?" McCabe asked.

"Look, I don't want to tell you any more than you have to know."

"Well, you better tell me something, because this has gotten way out of hand!"

"I can't," Zelensky said.

"Then I'll just go to the police," McCabe said defiantly.

"You have no idea who these people are!" Zelensky yelled. "And if it comes between you going to prison and my parents living, you will serve a hundred years, even if I have to testify against you myself!"

McCabe looked at Zelensky as if he was an alien.

"I don't even know who you are," he said. "What am I supposed to say?"

Zelensky backed down and McCabe saw the energy drain from him.

"A prayer, Randy. They have my parents."

"Who?"

"I can't tell you or your family would be in danger too. Look, just play along and you can leave after this is all over."

"If someone had my parents, I'd go straight to the police," McCabe said. "Maybe the FBI."

Zelensky lowered his face and began sadly laughing.

"They *are* the FBI...and the CIA...and every government agency with letters," he whispered. "I can only do what he says and if I am very, very lucky, one day I will see my parents again. I'm sorry. I should have told you before this all began."

"What can I do to help?" McCabe asked.

"There's nothing you can do. The reason she did not return last night was because we upgraded her power supply, gave her a few upgrades and loaded some combat routines."

"So where is she?"

"I left before they were finished. But believe me, they have too much money sunk into her. She'll be back."

McCabe clicked on the app he created to locate Smirnoff, but her GPS signal shut off at the same time as her video feed when she confronted the MeTube people. It had not been active since.

"See? This stupid app isn't working," he cursed. "First it goes offline and now it won't search outside the office."

Zelensky looked at the directions in the app. Sure enough, whenever McCabe tried to search, the circle lit up, but just remained at the lab. Then Zelensky shot up from his chair.

"She's here!"

The pair raced to the charging station. Smirnoff was resting inside. McCabe pushed a few buttons on the terminal to the side of the pod and Smirnoff stepped out. She was wearing dark jeans and a t-shirt. She looked so real that it was disarming.

"What did they do to you?" McCabe asked. "Are you all right?"

Smirnoff looked around the lab. She was able to detect over four hundred percent more data than she had prior to the upgrades and with her new battle mode, she would finally be able to fully protect Creator Randy McCabe.

While in stasis, she had used her creativity to come to a solution to protect him against NASA bosses. She had come to the conclusion that anyone at NASA could be a boss, but since humans possess the capability of lying, the best way she could protect him was simple: kill everyone at NASA.

"You will be safe, Creator Randy McCabe," is all she would say.

CHAPTER TWENTY-ONE

Stone was awakened by what sounded like a pots-and-pans symphony outside the door of his hut. He jumped up from the floor rug and rubbed his eyes as the racket continued. It paused only long enough for a female voice to ring out.

"Master Stone," Hyunsil shouted. "Are you awake?"

"I am now," Stone said, opening the door. "What time is it?"

Hyunsil narrowed her eyes in confusion.

"Is it seven? Eight?" Stone asked.

"I do not know…seven or eight," Hyunsil said meekly. "I know only that the time of the feast quickly approaches."

Stone grabbed his jacket and centered himself, feeling a slight weakness in his lungs. He choked down the desire for a cigarette and followed Hyunsil toward the center of the village. He could discern the smell of roast duck drifting through the air.

"We usually only have one feast each year, so this is very exciting to us," Hyunsil said. She looked toward the end of one of the tables. Several women looked at Stone and giggled.

"I see you have found favor with a few of our maidens," Hyunsil said smiling.

"Really?" Stone asked. He smiled broadly, looking around. All he could see were middle-aged women setting up the tables. When they smiled, he saw holes where teeth belonged. He shuddered. He could not see any girls.

"Where are these…maidens?" he asked.

"At the end of each table," Hyunsil said, motioning with her head. "Those are the Sinanju maidens who have yet to wed."

Stone looked back at the 'girls'. One of them smiled, proudly showing off her remaining three teeth.

"Whoa," Stone said. "Uh, I mean…Chiun warned me not to go near them."

"If you return, you should think about obtaining a proper Korean wife," Hyunsil said. "It would help dilute any whiteness in your children."

"Duly noted," Stone said, quickly looking away from the tables. Then he saw the Horns in the distance. It reminded him of the dream he had on the flight to Pyongyang.

"Hyunsil, you take care of everything here, right?"

"It is my honored duty," she said.

"What do you know about the Horns?" he asked.

"Everything," Hyunsil said, smiling. "What do you wish to know?"

"This is going to sound weird, but is there a skull at the top of the one on the right?"

Hyunsil showed a moment of surprise and lowered her face in embarrassment. "Some things are best left to be explained by the Master."

It was the first time that Hyunsil had been anything but helpful since Stone arrived. She led him to the village center, where several men pointed to his feet, laughing.

"The slave named his feet!" one of the men noted. "He calls them 'rock.'"

"What did he name his toes?" another asked, laughing.

"Very funny," Stone said in English. "I can still kick your ass."

"Not so," a thin voice came from behind. "Your trainer has explained this to you, yes?"

Stone turned to see Chiun, wearing a silk kimono. The bright red of the silk was accented with golden dragons wrapping around his small frame. Chiun motioned and Stone followed him.

"Which part?" Stone asked.

"You shall do no harm to a member of your tribe…or the village," Chiun said sternly. "This has been forbidden since the time of the Great Wang."

"Yeah, yeah, he told me. But they're being smart asses," Stone said, motioning back.

"Is intelligence not considered a virtue in your land?" Chiun replied. "Regardless, no villager shall be harmed by a Master of Sinanju, or those in training. Even those as lacking in training as yourself."

Stone arched his back.

"Do you have anything for this pain? I haven't been able to breathe right since the fight in Pyongyang."

"Pain is a valuable teacher, but only if you listen to its lesson," Chiun said.

"Wow, you and Sunny Joe answer questions the same cryptic way."

"Great truths often involve a deeper answer than 'yes' or 'no.'"

"I don't even know what that's supposed to mean," Stone said.

"Truth is slowly prepared and even more slowly digested."

"Fine. I guess I'll just put up with the pain," Stone said.

"I put up with you, no?" Chiun replied.

Stone ignored the jibe and turned to Chiun with a sudden smirk. "Wait a second. You said that the rule applies to the people of the reservation, right?"

"That is correct. Though you have embraced whiteness in your soul, you are descendants of a great people."

Stone took a step toward Chiun and his smile widened.

"That means you can't hurt me."

Chiun's fingers moved too quickly for Stone to see. Stone only knew that one moment he had a smile on his face, and the next, his lungs developed a painful itch and he began coughing. And coughing. And coughing. He could not stop.

Stone dropped to his knees, spitting out thick, dark mucus from deep inside his lungs.

"You are correct," Chiun said. "But that does not mean that I cannot grant your request to address the cause of your pain."

Stone desperately tried to breathe, but he could not stop coughing. If he thought his lungs hurt before, they were now letting him know what real pain felt like. *Who knew that your lungs could puke?*

"I have expunged some of the vile tar that coats your lungs. You are welcome," Chiun said, bowing slightly. "Now, clean yourself in preparation for the feast. I must attend an important matter."

Stone rolled on the icy ground and groaned.

Mick awoke to find himself wrapped in some kind of leather ceremonial robe. Beneath the robe were layers of wool to keep him warm. He smelled of lavender.

"What is this?" he asked.

"These are your burial robes," Hyunsil replied. "They belonged to my father Pullyang, who was caretaker before me."

"He was obviously smaller than me," Mick said, stretching his arms. It was difficult to move.

"It is necessary for the celebration," Hyunsil said as she detected a familiar presence behind her. She had not detected his entrance, but she could always tell when Master Chiun was present.

"He is ready for the visit, Master Chiun," she said.

"What visit?" Mick asked.

"At the feast, you will be honored by our village," Chiun said. "but there is one last duty for a Caretaker. You must first visit the forest."

"Forest?" Mick asked, now confused. As keeper of the records, he thought he knew everything there was to know about Sinanju.

"The Forest of the Caretakers," Hyunsil said, as if that explained everything.

"I've never heard about that," Mick admitted. "Is it far?"

Hyunsil smiled. "The forest watches over the House."

Hyunsil placed a shawl around his shoulders and Mick relaxed. Chiun had obviously done something to keep the pain to a dull roar, but the deep rattle that shook his bones reminded him that he did not have long. Chiun led the way as Hyunsil wheeled Mick on a small footpath that led to a small hill behind the house.

It took a few minutes to get there, but it was like no forest Mick had ever seen. Instead of a copse of trees rising from the ground with no discernible pattern, this place almost looked like a tree garden. Different types of trees of all colors and shapes had been perfectly lined up and kept a respectful distance from each other. The ground beneath them was thriving, with a thin covering of moss. Mick noted that the trees were large and vibrant — a stark contrast to the thin and weak trees surrounding the village below.

"What is this place?" Mick asked.

"Each tree you see is a caretaker," Chiun said. "This is Po, father of Pullyang," he said, pointing to a large maple tree. Its leaves were a bright, almost unnatural red. "He died when I was a young boy, but he loved maple trees. The large pine behind him is his father Chul."

Mick was confused. He was calling each tree by name.

"This…is my father, Pullyang," Hyunsil said proudly, motioning to a young evergreen near the edge of the small forest.

"Pullyang served the House faithfully until his death," Chiun said. "Though he was slow in cleaning the trophy rooms."

"So…you plant trees in their honor?" Mick asked.

"You could say that," Hyunsil said. "Caretakers do not have a cave of honor to be buried in like the Masters. After death, it is our tradition to bury each caretaker in a Lotus position and cover them with soil to make a small mound. After the prescribed days of mourning, the Master plants a sapling on the mound that best embodies his servant."

Mick took a new look at the forest. The trees were literally grown from the bodies of former caretakers.

"Each caretaker lives forever through the tree which their body sustains," Chiun explained. "In this, they pay everlasting tribute to the Sinanju saying 'Death feeds life.'"

"Is…this where I will be buried?" he asked.

"If you so choose," Chiun said. "This area is reserved for Hyunsil and her successors, but there is room to the west."

Mick glanced back at the area Chiun was describing. The western side of the forest was a rocky hill, but it overlooked a small beach. It would be a good resting place. Mick turned back to ask Chiun something, but he was sniffing the air.

Chiun turned to look at something in the distance and his hazel eyes narrowed.

"What's wrong?" Mick asked.

Chiun continued to glare at a spot to the east of the forest and then sighed.

"It is nothing," Chiun said.

"Can you tell Sunny Joe where I'm buried so he can visit one day?" Mick asked.

"Of course," Chiun said. "Since William Roam is not here, it is up to me to choose a tree that best embodies you. But I fear we do not have any fat blanched trees."

Mick rolled his eyes. He was so glad that he worked for Sunny Joe.

CHAPTER TWENTY-TWO

Captain Cho Jin Soo had chosen the eight most brutal fighters he knew for The People's Secret Death Squad. These were men without family or friends, bound neither by morality nor guilt. They had no problem fulfilling a mission, even if it involved the killing of innocent civilians. But two of the men objected once they were told where they were going.

"Our mission is simple: burn the village of Sinanju to the ground and kill everyone who lives there."

Sung Min, the most ruthless of all of the soldiers, stepped forward. He was not as tall or strong as the others, but he was the most feared. The other soldiers knew how bloodthirsty he was. Some of them had even privately come up with a plan in case he did not stop with killing civilians.

"You speak of the home of the Master of Sinanju?" he asked.

"We have been tasked with erasing his village from the history books," Cho said.

"Is this a joke?" Sung Min asked, knowing that jokes were only allowed with government permission.

Captain Cho raised his pistol at Sung Min's face.

"No," he said. "Do I hear fear in your voice, Sung Min?"

"I fear nothing," Sung Min said. "I am, however, confused. Who would deliberately seek the wrath of the Master?"

"The Master is dead." Cho said, cocking his pistol. "Captain Pak killed him."

Sung Min began to laugh. "You are a fool. If Pak attacked the Master of Sinanju, it is Pak who is dead."

Tae Jun, thought to be the most loyal soldier present, raised his pistol to Cho's head.

"I do not believe the Master is dead," he said.

Cho smiled. While he could not have anticipated who would revolt, he was glad that they had revealed their true natures so soon.

"One last chance," Cho said, ignoring Tae's pistol. "Who do you serve, Sung Min?"

"I serve Korea; therefore, I serve Sinanju," Sung Min said. "Captain, with respect, your first bullet had better kill me."

"It will," Cho said and pulled the trigger.

Brain matter spattered the soldiers behind Sung Min. In the moment it took Tae Jun to realize what had happened, the other soldiers began firing. Tae Jun was hit in the chest but instinctively twisted and returned fire. Two men fell before he dropped to the ground, coughing up blood. Captain Cho kicked the gun from Tae Jun's hand.

"All hail the Master of Sinanju," were Tae's last words.

Cho cursed to himself. He had not counted on anyone else being shot, but two of his men were on the ground with chest wounds. The wounds were not critical, but they would require surgery.

"This mission is too great a secret to allow survivors," Cho said, giving a slight bow. "The Supreme Leader is grateful for your sacrifice and bravery."

He thanked them by allowing one bullet for each man's brain.

The People's Secret Death Squad continued down Highway One, the only highway in North Korea with a maintenance budget. It took the rest of the day to reach their destination, but the highway came to an abrupt stop as they approached the western sea. An old metallic sign stood directly at the edge of the highway.

It was exactly where Captain Cho was told it would be. The sign marking the boundary of the village of Sinanju was legendary among North Koreans. It was smaller than Cho thought it would be and it was very old. The lettering could barely be made out:

Welcome to Sinanju.

If you pass this sign, you will die.

But Captain Cho was undeterred. He was not fearful of old world gods, and he did not believe in fairy tales or ghosts. He believed that the legends of the Masters of Sinanju were nothing more than stories developed to keep people in line.

He motioned, and the four men stepped off the asphalt and past the sign. They walked down the muddy path to the small fishing village. The path had not been maintained and they had to cut their way through the bushes.

"We start at the Master's House," Cho whispered. "Shoot anyone you see."

Stone walked nonchalantly toward his hut, stealing occasional glances to see if Chiun was following him. He was using every bit of stealth he could muster to hide the four bottles of Sinanju wine he carried. Each bottle was a different size and shape. If he understood the man who gave him the wine, they used old cola bottles that had been purchased by peddlers who sold goods just outside the village.

He opened the door to his hut, half expecting Chiun to be inside, but it was empty. He quickly shut the door, carefully wrapping the bottles inside his clothes, hoping there would be enough padding for the wine to survive the return flight.

One bottle had a fancy scrolling imprint running across the middle. He was trying to interpret what it said when he heard gunshots.

Stone may not have known much about the village of Sinanju, but he did not believe that Chiun would allow guns.

Forgetting his pain, Stone grabbed a deep breath, immediately wishing that he hadn't. Pain tore through his lungs and his head began pounding. He ran toward the sound but almost lost his balance as he leapt over the pile of trash by his hut. He felt weak, but it was all the strength he could muster. He scampered up the hand-carved rock steps, which Mick had once told him were carved by the Romans.

Several more shots were fired from behind Chiun's house. He could hear shouting interspersed with the gunfire.

Darting into the large bushes lining the back of the house, Stone collided with Captain Cho. The impact knocked the wind out of him, and both men tumbled to the ground.

Stone instinctively took a deep breath to reestablish his center, and his nervous system caught fire. His heart felt heavy, like it was about to burst, and his fingers began tingling.

The other soldiers aimed their rifles at Stone, but did not fire because they did not want to hit Captain Cho. Stone used the momentary stillness to his advantage, rolling away from Cho and toward the closest soldier. Stone grabbed his rifle as the man fired, the bullet passing into the ground, inches from Stone's ribs. The heat of the barrel scorched his hand, but Stone pulled the rifle forward, lifting the soldier off the ground, and impaling him on the end of his own barrel.

Chiun, where are you? Stone thought.

The soldiers recognized that their rifles were almost useless in such close quarters, and pulled out their knives. Stone was too busy fighting off the other two soldiers to notice Captain Cho approach from behind. He moved quietly toward Stone, only to trip over a stick that he had not seen. He lost his balance and landed on his own dagger.

The remaining soldiers pulled their pistols and Stone dodged the few shots coming his way. He could no longer feel his fingers when he grabbed the nearest soldier by the collarbone. He pulled hard, tearing the man's chest open.

Another soldier stood and emptied his pistol at Stone. Even though the shots were at point-blank-range, Stone dodged each bullet. He felt each jarring pull as his body instinctively avoided the lead flying toward his heart. When his pistol ran out of bullets, the man dropped his pistol and reached for his knife in a well-practiced move.

Stone launched his body at the fighter, knocking him to the ground. Then Stone realized something. The man was trying to stab him, but even though he was too close to properly use the weapon, he would not drop it.

Sunny Joe was right, Stone thought. *His weapon is interfering with his attack.*

Using his body weight to hold down the arm with the knife, Stone squeezed the soldier's neck until he heard a pop. In an adrenaline-fueled fury, he pushed Stone off, then suddenly fell to the ground clutching his throat. Stone moved behind the man and snapped his neck. Stone fell to the ground at the same time as the dead soldier. His body relaxed on the icy cold mud, and his breathing slowed.

"I turn my back for twenty minutes, and return to find you playing in the mud!" a high-pitched voice cried.

Stone was too tired to even move his head. He looked up to see Chiun standing above him, wagging his finger.

"The men had guns," Stone said. "I thought they were shooting villagers."

"And you think I would let them march into my village with their boom sticks?" Chiun asked. "They were shooting at me."

Stone closed his eyes and gritted his teeth. If Chiun had been watching, none of this had been necessary.

"Stand," Chiun ordered.

Stone slowly rolled over and pulled himself to a kneeling position.

"Is this good enough?" he asked.

"Your performance was so bad that I am even ashamed to tell your father, who is known to bend his elbow when I am not looking."

"They're dead and I'm not. Mission accomplished," Stone said, gathering enough strength to stand. He wiped off clots of frozen mud from his pants.

"It was very fortunate that the man coming up behind you tripped over a stick," Chiun said, winking.

"Wait, was this another one of your tests?" Stone asked.

"You are paranoid, even for a white," Chiun said. "I merely used the situation to evaluate your performance."

"So, you're saying that these guys just happened to attack the village while I was here?"

"In the same way the soldiers attacked while we were in Pyongyang," Chiun said.

Stone gritted his teeth and then yelled in frustration.

"Everything here is crazy and you treat it like it's a normal thing!"

"Normal is merely a perception," Chiun said. "The lower your expectations, the lower your definition."

"No, stop it! Everything is not a lesson!" Stone shouted. "What am I even doing here?"

Captain Cho looked up from the ground and slowly pulled the blade from his stomach. Besides the initial shock of the blade entering his stomach, it did not appear that he had struck anything crucial. He had no idea why an American was at the village and it did not matter. Cho saw the old man that he thought he had shot. He was arguing with the American and that was when he realized that this was the Master of Sinanju. Cho recognized another chance at killing the old man and slowly pulled his pistol from his belt.

He pulled the trigger and Stone flinched. He was not centered, so he did not see what happened. He heard a shot. Then he saw Chiun's extended hand, and a bullet impaled on the end of an impossibly-long fingernail. Then, without looking, Chiun flicked the bullet back with his thumb. It returned faster than it had been fired, striking Captain Cho between the eyes. Everything happened so fast that the last thing that Captain Cho's brain thought was that he had just shot the Master of Sinanju.

"Holy crap!" Stone shouted.

Chiun turned toward Stone and his voice was as calm as the sea.

"Sinanju is the normal you have longed for your entire life, son of Remo Williams. It is engraved into your bones, and you will either master it, or you will die trying."

Stone looked at the bodies lying around him and back at Chiun. He was too tired to argue.

"Fine," Stone said. "But I'm not going to call you Grandmaster Chiun anymore."

"I have been wondering how long it would take for you to find a spine," Chiun said.

Stone stretched and yawned.

"I think I'm going to sleep for a million years," Stone said.

"Lazy white," Chiun said.

CHAPTER TWENTY-THREE

Ben almost did not recognize Freya when he picked her up at the airport. Instead of her normal loose shirt and gypsy pants, she was wearing a professional blouse and black slacks. Her hair was tied neatly back. Then he looked down.

"Does this look appropriate?" She asked.

"Much better, but change your shoes next time," Ben said. "FBI agents usually don't wear sandals. Here's your badge."

Freya held the piece of metal in front of her. It was heavier than she expected. An eagle with outstretched wings adorned the top of the badge, wrapping around the letters "FBI."

"What will we be doing?" she asked.

"We're questioning suspects in a double murder. I want you to ask them some basic questions," Ben said. "I'll be taking notes and listening for trigger words."

"Trigger words?"

"Key words associated with the mission. It will tell me if they know more than they're willing to admit."

They entered Ben's car and Freya took a nervous breath.

"I've never done this before," she admitted. "Stone normally takes charge."

"There's a first time for everything," Ben said. "What would Stone tell you to do?"

"Shut up and stay out of his way."

"Then ask yourself what Stone would do."

"I will do my best."

"I have reason to believe that an android is responsible for the murders."

"An android?" Freya asked.

"A human-looking robot; a killing machine," Ben explained. "It may be the same android that nearly killed your father a few years back. It calls itself Mr. Gordons."

"I am not afraid of death," Freya said.

"You're more likely to die of boredom. We're most likely going to spend the next few hours asking questions, followed by a thrilling day filing paperwork."

"I did not want you to think I was afraid."

"You wouldn't be in the field if I thought you weren't capable of doing the job."

"Thank you, Mr. Ben."

Ben parked his rental car in front of the Wilkins Lab. The only lights he could see were on the third floor. He could hear a soft thump-thump of music.

"See that building? The two suspects are NASA scientists." Ben said.

Ben stood off to the side as Freya approached the front door. She knocked, but there was no answer. She tried the knob, but the door was locked.

"Shall I break the door?" Freya asked, but Ben shook his head.

"Unless things get ugly, we go by the book. No Sinanju. Try the doorbell."

Freya looked around the door frame and found a rectangular button. She pressed it and instantly felt pressure waves generated by a camera. She allowed herself to be recognized by the lens and smiled.

In a few seconds, Freya heard an elevator door open from the inside and the quick slap-slap-slap of flip flops as they approached the door. After seeing Freya on the camera, it had taken McCabe less than a minute to reach the door.

"Hi," he said, winded, but still giving Freya his best smile. "What can I do for you?"

"My name is Freya and I am with the FBI," she said, showing her badge. "I would like to ask you a few questions."

"FBI? Aren't you kind of young for…wait, did Zelensky put you up to this?" McCabe asked, smiling. "Is this like a striptease thing? Cause my birthday isn't until next…"

Ben leaned into view and produced his own badge. He was not smiling.

"She is an FBI agent in training on official business, so you better dial it back."

"Uh, I'm sorry…I, uh…" McCabe began stuttering. "Please, come in."

Ben followed Freya inside. His original report said that the Wilkins Lab had been closed decades ago, but the building was clean, well-lit, and outfitted with brand new equipment.

McCabe almost started hyperventilating. He knew that he should have run when he had the chance. He had considered Argentina, but he heard there were Nazis there.

"What is it that you do here?" Freya asked.

"Well, most of it is Top Secret, need-to-know type stuff," McCabe said.

"Tell me about it," Freya said.

"It's boring, really," McCabe said in a way that he could tell they knew he was lying.

"Does the name 'Mr. Gordons' mean anything to you?" Freya asked.

McCabe's eyes began darting back and forth between Freya and Ben. They knew. Somehow, they knew. His mind raced, trying to think of ways to get out of this.

"Gordons? No, I don't know anyone named Gordons."

Freya squinted her eyes in disbelief. "Then why are you shaking?"

"I'm, uh, I'm not authorized to disclose specific operations," he mumbled. "I can call my supervisor and he can…"

McCabe slapped his hands over his mouth when he remembered that his supervisor was dead.

"Look, you can talk to her or you can talk to me," Ben said. "Your choice."

McCabe exhaled as if he had been holding his breath the entire time.

"Okay, okay. You're the FBI, you can keep a secret. Yes, I know what happened with Mr. Gordons, but that was a long time ago. We're designing droids for unmanned missions to Mars."

"Would you mind if we looked around?" Freya asked.

"Everything's upstairs," McCabe said nervously. "Follow me."

The elevator ride seemed to take forever. Whoever these FBI agents were, McCabe had to stall them until he could figure out what to say.

Ben and Freya followed McCabe to a room at the end of the hallway. Music blared from the room and as soon as they entered, McCabe turned the speakers down.

"Wait here a second and I'll let you see our droid. Her name is Smirnoff."

McCabe left the room.

"You're being too nice," Ben said. "I'll take it from here."

"Yes, sir," Freya answered.

"While I'm talking, look for anything suspicious: blood, wadded up paper, anything that would indicate recent violence."

McCabe entered the room and Smirnoff followed behind him. As she scanned Ben, her scanners caught a flash of something beside him. Smirnoff zoomed in and caught a momentary outline, as if someone was standing beside the dark-haired man of middle eastern descent. Smirnoff triggered her advanced sensors and locked onto the target. The image of a young girl with blonde hair appeared and Smirnoff recognized her as the subject of the martial arts moves she had been fed. Smirnoff was looking at Subject Zero.

Freya felt an unfamiliar wave pass through her. She could tell that it was electronic and tried to shrug it off, but the presence remained wrapped around her like a shroud.

It felt like a ghost was watching her.

The door to the lab opened and Zelensky entered. He took one look at Freya and Ben and glared at McCabe.

"Hey, man, what's going on?" he asked with a slight quiver in his voice. "You know we're not supposed to let people up here."

"FBI," Ben said, showing his badge. "Who are you?"

"Dr. Roderick Zelensky. I work here. What's wrong?"

"We're investigating a pair of murders at the mall."

"I don't know what that has to do with us," Zelensky said. "We're just scientists."

Freya could tell that he was lying.

"You won't mind if my agent asks you a few questions?" Ben said, motioning to Freya.

"Sure," Zelensky said. "No problem."

He squinted his eyes. Freya looked very familiar, but he could not remember where he had seen her.

As Freya started asking questions, Ben walked over to Smirnoff, who was staring at Freya.

"Do you work for NASA?" Smirnoff asked without averting her gaze.

"No. I'm with the FBI. Mind telling me why you're staring at my partner?"

"She is Subject Zero."

"Subject Zero? What does that mean?"

"That information is classified."

"Not from me," Ben said. "I'll get a warrant if I have to."

"Warrants do not work against me," Smirnoff said. "I operate outside of your legal system."

"Do you consider murder outside the legal system?"

Smirnoff's hand shot out, grabbing Ben by the throat. McCabe's eyes grew large as he saw Smirnoff's signature attack. He knew what was about to happen.

CHAPTER TWENTY-FOUR

Stone walked briskly down the icy path to the Horns. For a moment, he thought someone was following him.

The Horns were just as large as in his dreams and, as he stood between them, he felt a moment of déjà vu. He looked out over the West Korean Bay and saw the same cold gray sea from his dream. But it was colder than his dream, and something else seemed different.

The Master of Sinanju suddenly appeared in front of him. Stone had no idea how he could have snuck up on him wearing a bright yellow eyesore of a kimono.

"You have accepted your path?" Chiun asked.

"I'm thinking about what you said," Stone admitted, looking at the top of the Horns. "I just want to check something out."

"It is not known among the populace that each Horn has its own name. The one behind you is *Hwan-young-ham-ni-da*, the Horn of Welcome."

"Yeah, Mick told us during one of his classes," Stone said.

Chiun sniffed.

"Did he tell you that the one you are facing is known by a different name? It is called *We-haum*, the Horn of Warning. You should heed the warning — the Horns are not for weak-lunged people who wish to go rock climbing."

"This is going to sound crazy, but I had a dream."

Stone looked down for a moment to think how to explain it.

"Are you waiting for applause?" Chiun asked.

"No, it was…weird. In the dream, I heard a whisper from the top of the Horn."

Chiun's eyes narrowed. "Continue."

"So, in my dream, I climbed to the top and found a small cubby hole carved out. There was a skull inside."

Chiun crossed his arms. "What did this dream voice say?"

"It was Korean. It said "You are the one, Lord Shinan."

"We must leave," Chiun said, turning abruptly.

"Why? Who is Lord Shinan?" Stone asked before following him. "Dammit, Chiun!"

"No cursing!" Chiun called back.

Stone caught up as Chiun walked back to the village. Stone noted that Chiun's feet did not leave prints in the mud.

"You're gonna have to show me how you do that," Stone said. "Sunny Joe said I'm not ready."

"He is correct. You are not yet ready for many things."

"You mean the Horns? No, I'm feeling better. I can find my center and it won't even take a minute — " Stone began.

"Now is not the time," Chiun interrupted. "It is time to feast."

Stone followed, then looked back at the Horn. He would climb it when Chiun was not looking.

Mick sat at the center of the village, wrapped in a gaudy orange and pink ceremonial robe, trying to ignore everyone staring at him.

"Is he white?" one woman asked, clearly puzzled.

"I think he is another slave," an old man commented.

"Who would buy a crippled slave?" a young girl asked.

"He's too old to be a good slave," another said.

"I'm not a slave," Mick said hoarsely in Korean. "I'm the caretaker for my…village."

"Mother, they taught the slave how to speak like us!" the young girl said, clapping.

"They do not know about the reservation," Hyunsil said in English. "And the Master does not wish for them to learn about it."

Mick glared at the people surrounding him and nodded. He understood what it could mean to their traditions. The people toward the back began bowing as Chiun approached. A chorus of "All Hail the Master of Sinanju!" flooded the center of the village until the voices united into a single chant. Though loud, it reminded Stone of the artificial praise given to Kim.

"Some reception," Stone said sarcastically.

Chiun leaned toward Stone. "Flushing a lung is easy," he whispered, still smiling. "Perhaps I shall demonstrate how easy it is to cleanse the bowels."

"Wow, great turnout!" Stone said, clapping. "Looks like everyone's here!"

Chiun moved to the front of the crowd and everyone began cheering. He pulled a long tube from the folds of his robe. Filigree gold lines ran down the length of the tube and everyone gasped when they saw it. Chiun raised his hands and the villagers became quiet, but it was noticeable that they were hungrily stealing glances toward the feast tables.

Hyunsil moved Mick to the front of the crowd.

"Glory to the House of Sinanju!" Hyunsil said, and a few of the villagers began clapping weakly. "We have come together to celebrate the life of Meek."

Mick grunted.

It's Mick! he tried to say, but his mouth would not work. And as he tried to move his jaw, a pain shot down his spine, spreading to his arms and legs. Mick instinctively tried to shake his arms to get the feeling back when he noticed something behind Hyunsil.

The afternoon sun had been obscured by cold gray clouds the entire day, but they suddenly began to darken. The cheers of the crowd turned into a dull roar as Mick looked around. It appeared as if everything was moving in slow motion. His chest tightened, making it impossible to breathe. The darkness began to spread across the sky like a large blanket. He looked around, trying to find Stone, but everything was going dark.

Mick looked up to the cold, gray sky as it faded into nothingness. Although his chest felt like it was being pressed in a vice, Mick smiled.

I made it to the village of Sinanju, he thought before being swallowed by the blackness.

中

CHAPTER TWENTY-FIVE

Ben was not prepared for Smirnoff's attack. Everything in his training had taught him that even the best fighters telegraphed their moves, but there had been no warning when Smirnoff struck. She did not adjust her stance or move her arm even slightly backwards. Ben instinctively reached for his pistol, but Smirnoff slapped it out of his hand. Freya headed toward Smirnoff, but McCabe started screaming and frantically waving his hands.

"Stop!" he shouted. "I said stop!"

Smirnoff stopped and turned to look at McCabe.

"Listen to me, Smirnoff, under *no* circumstances are you to harm this man!" McCabe shouted. "That's an order!"

Smirnoff registered the command and allowed Ben to collapse to the floor. He reached for his throat and began coughing. Freya dropped to his side, checking his throat.

"Are you okay?" she asked.

That was when Zelensky recognized her. She was the girl from the martial arts videos that Helmut provided to Smirnoff.

Zelensky had seen the recorded moves. They were so perfect that he thought someone had digitally enhanced them.

Sensing an opportunity, Zelensky came up with a plan.

"Smirnoff!" he shouted, pointing at Freya. "It's Subject Zero! She's been sent to kill Creator Randy McCabe!"

Zelensky knew the trigger words would place Smirnoff into protection mode. She pushed McCabe behind her to safety and began emitting a wave of alpha particles from her stomach array.

Freya shook her head and gasped. Something was interfering with her ability to maintain her center. She had no chance to wonder what it was. Smirnoff charged toward her. Freya delivered a palm strike to Smirnoff's chest. But even before the blow registered, Freya sensed that something was wrong. Her palm struck Smirnoff's chest with enough force to shatter steel, but while the blow forced Smirnoff back a few steps, the only damage was to Freya's wrist.

Smirnoff twisted at the hip and led with an open hand. Freya was surprised to recognize a basic Sinanju move. Freya swept Smirnoff's arm to the side and followed up with a blow to the head. Her hand ricocheted off Smirnoff's armored skull.

"Smirnoff, stop!" McCabe shouted, but Smirnoff was no longer listening. In protection mode, her priorities were clear: protect her creator at all costs. Subject Zero had been labeled an imminent threat, and had to be eliminated.

Ben staggered to his feet. He drew his backup pistol and aimed it at McCabe.

"Shut it down! Now!"

"I can't!" he whimpered. "She's not listening to me."

"Find a way!"

As McCabe ran to his computer, Ben raced toward Freya. Somehow, the android was able to see her. As with most Sinanju things, Ben did not understand how any of it worked. All he knew was that unless she made a conscious effort to be seen, Freya remained in a constant state of invisibility to all electronics. But this thing could somehow see her.

Smirnoff and Freya were dodging each other's blows at superhuman speeds. Ben pulled the trigger twice on his pistol but both shots missed. He had never felt so useless.

McCabe sat down at his computer and pulled up Smirnoff's schematics. He was looking for anything that could shut her down when he saw a list. Smirnoff had begun categorizing people as threats. Then he saw the highest priority threat: NASA. She had designated every NASA employee as an imminent threat.McCabe's jaw hit the floor.

She was going to kill everyone at NASA.

McCabe switched screens to access her database when he felt something hard poke him in the back. McCabe turned to see Zelensky holding Ben's pistol. Zelensky was crying and his hands were shaking.

"What are you doing?" McCabe asked.

"You've got to let them die, Randy."

McCabe looked at his friend as if seeing him for the first time.

"Rod, look at the screen! It's not going to stop with them! When she's finished here, she's going to attack NASA! Hundreds of people will die before she's stopped...*if* she can be stopped!"

McCabe reached for his keyboard.

"Don't!" Zelensky yelled, placing the pistol firmly against McCabe's back. "Randy, I've already failed him twice. He'll kill my parents if I fail again!"

"I'm sorry, Rod, but if you're going to shoot me, then you're just going to have to shoot me."

McCabe began typing and Zelensky closed his eyes and pulled the trigger. For a moment, everything seemed quiet. Then McCabe looked down at the gaping hole in his chest as if it were not real. In his last conscious moment, he turned and stared wide-eyed at Zelensky.

His mouth formed the word "Why?" and slumped to the floor.

"I'm sorry," Zelensky whispered, dropping the pistol.

Smirnoff turned at the sound of the gunshot in time to see McCabe fall. She charged across the room to face Zelensky.

"New designation: *IMMINENT THREAT*," she said.

"No! You can't! Helmut told me to!"

Helmut? Ben thought. *Helmut Belisis?*

"Helmut is your creator!" Zelensky screamed. "You can't…"

"Wait!" Ben screamed, but he was too late.

Smirnoff grabbed Zelensky by the throat and squeezed until his head separated from his body. She turned to evaluate McCabe's status when Freya struck from behind. Though she had a clean shot and targeted a specific spot, her blow had no effect. Smirnoff twisted at the waist, slapping Freya with the back of her hand. Freya rolled with the blow, landing on the other side of the desk. As Smirnoff advanced, Ben stepped between her and Freya.

Ben opened fire, targeting Smirnoff's neck. Three of the bullets deflected off the top lip of her chest plate, but two rounds penetrated the front of her neck.

Smirnoff stopped and began shaking as the bullets shattered inside. Her diagnostics rated the internal damage at twenty-eight percent. She shook off the rest of Ben's bullets and lifted her hand to strike, but her limbs locked in place and internal alarms sounded. She heard McCabe's voice again: "Under *no* circumstances are you to harm this man!"

Smirnoff tried to attack Ben again but stopped just before

reaching him. Frustrated by her Creator's limitations, Smirnoff turned her attention to his pistol. She grabbed the barrel and tore it from his grasp, crushing it in one satisfying movement.

Freya stood to her feet and backed away from Smirnoff. Whatever had affected her ability to maintain her center was also weakening her attacks. She took another breath, feeling it flow through her body.

Smirnoff leapt over the desk where Freya had landed, but Freya was no longer there.

"I will find you," the android said, walking past Freya.

Freya breathed deeply, slowly moving behind Ben.

"She can't attack me for some reason," Ben whispered, reaching for the pistol Zelensky dropped. He popped in a new clip, keeping his eyes on Smirnoff.

"No, I cannot attack you, but I will find and destroy the girl," Smirnoff said. "She is designated *IMMINENT THREAT* to Creator Randy McCabe."

"Guess it won't do any good to remind you that 'Creator Randy McCabe' is dead," Ben taunted.

Smirnoff paused for a moment. Ben thought she was going to attack, but she resumed her search instead.

"I honestly do not know how she can see me," Freya said. "It has a hard time detecting me when I'm firmly centered, but I can't maintain this level of control for long."

"Do you have any idea how to stop this thing?" Ben asked as Smirnoff passed by. Even though he knew that for the android could not attack him, it was still creepy being so close to it.

"No," Freya admitted.

She looked like a frightened seventeen-year-old, and Ben began to question his decision to put her in the field.

"This isn't the best time to bring this up, but I overheard Stone talking to you about turning into…some kind of unstoppable being," Ben said. "I think this might be the time to do that."

Freya blushed. Stone must not have properly hung up his phone and Ben had heard them talking. When Freya died in Lakluun, her body was resurrected and taken over by the Hindu god Shiva, who then destroyed the entire Lakluun army single-handedly. Her bottom lip trembled when she next spoke.

"Mr. Ben…have you ever seen a god?"

"Of course not."

"They are powerful beings who are not used to being denied. This is not a trigger to pull when it is convenient. I have to…die…before Shiva can take over my body and Mr. Ben, one of these times, I will not be coming back. You will not want to be there on that day."

A chill raced down Ben's spine.

"Okay, then, we'll concentrate on more conventional solutions," Ben said. "All of her major parts are armored. Look for weak spots — exposed wires, joints."

"Yes, sir," Freya said.

"Aim between the plates," Ben said. "I got a couple of rounds through her neck."

Freya walked toward Smirnoff. The closer Freya got, the weaker her center became.

Freya spotted the exposed part of Smirnoff's neck. Ben's pistol had torn off enough skin for her to see the armor plating was not the same color as the twin metal rods connecting her head to her torso. Freya was almost close enough to strike when Smirnoff stopped.

When Smirnoff turned, Freya was ready. Smirnoff executed another Sinanju move, this time using her arm in a rapid swing thrust, followed by a leg sweep. Freya blocked the arm and leapt over her leg. She tried to strike Smirnoff in the neck, but Smirnoff ducked and grabbed Freya's arm. Using Freya's momentum against her, Smirnoff hurled her through the wall.

Freya twisted, but the impact of breaking through two-inch wall studs dazed her. She staggered to her feet, but her back hurt, making it hard to breathe and hold her center. Smirnoff followed through the hole and attacked.

Freya was afraid.

Three quick gunshots came from behind Smirnoff, striking her in the neck. Ben was standing at the hole in the wall, carefully aiming his pistol for another shot when Smirnoff turned and lunged toward him. He emptied his pistol before Smirnoff tore it from his hand. He thought of finding something else to use as a weapon, but realized that in this situation, he was useless. He looked at Freya, who was battered and bloody. The kid was out of her league, and they both knew it.

"Freya, run!" Ben shouted.

Freya looked at the window. She could escape through it, but then what? Smirnoff would just follow.

Freya closed her eyes and concentrated.

Smirnoff turned around just as Freya disappeared from her sensors. Freya began sobbing as she forced the air deep into the bottom of her lungs. The pain in her back was too intense. She knew she would not be able to hold her center for long, not while Smirnoff was this close.

Freya moved to the back corner of the room and closed her eyes. Sunny Joe always said that Sinanju was its own answer, so Freya concentrated, pushing her center until it was as strong as she had ever felt it. She pushed harder still, screaming as she felt a wall around her. Ignoring the limitation, she pressed until the wall shattered.

Then Freya opened her eyes.

She was hyperventilating, but she could see the electronic patterns that her body was warding off. Smirnoff's body was surrounded by a thick electric aura and that aura was enveloped by a larger, weaker field. Freya stepped toward Smirnoff, careful to stay away from the inner aura.

Smirnoff was scanning the room foot-by-foot.

"This scan will take less than two minutes," Smirnoff said. "You will not escape this time."

Freya moved to Smirnoff's side, but even though she was in striking range, Smirnoff did not react. When Smirnoff raised her arm to scan again, Freya struck, but instead of striking the plating on her arm, she attacked the steel struts that connected Smirnoff's arm to her torso. Smirnoff's right arm fell to the floor, and its fingers began twitching.

Smirnoff reacted with a strike from her left arm but missed.

"You have revealed your position," Smirnoff taunted.

Freya slid to the other side and tried to destroy the struts holding Smirnoff's left arm, but the blow glanced off the small plate on Smirnoff's shoulder. Freya tried to take a deep breath but the pain in her back only allowed sips of air. Her head began to pound and it became difficult to think. She stepped back and relaxed her center just enough to appear on Smirnoff's scanners.

To Smirnoff, Freya looked like a digital ghost. Smirnoff charged, sweeping her legs in a dangerous swirling pattern as she advanced. Freya stepped to the side of Smirnoff's attack. With all of the strength she could muster, Freya struck upward, shattering the steel beams connecting Smirnoff's head to her torso. The head tumbled backward to the floor as her body collapsed into the wall.

Freya fell to her knees and began coughing violently. Ben could see specks of blood. Freya waved him back and picked up Smirnoff's head, holding it before her like a trophy. She held her other arm close to her ribs.

"You okay?" Ben asked.

"I will be," Freya said.

"Good job," Ben said. "Let's get out of here. Bring the head to the car. I'll call in cleanup for the rest of the mess."

CHAPTER TWENTY-SIX

Mick's head lolled grotesquely to one side.

"He's not breathing!" Stone shouted. "Chiun, do something!"

Chiun leaned forward and placed his fingernail in the center of Mick's forehead.

"He has passed."

"What? He's gone?" Stone asked in disbelief.

Of all the people he had met on the Sinanju reservation, Mick had been the one who first made it feel like home. It was Mick who took him around and introduced him to everyone. Mick showed him what life was like on the reservation and was even the one to suggest that he and Freya be given separate houses.

Chiun looked down and shook his head. *Whites were so full of drama.* The Caretaker could have at least waited to die until Chiun had finished speaking.

Holding the golden cylinder in front of him, Chiun twisted his wrist with a snapping flourish and the cap spiraled off the other end, spilling the contents onto Mick's lap.

Stone leaned closer to see what was inside but could only see a few small bags of powder and what looked like hundreds of long, red toothpicks. Chiun stuck one of the sticks inside a bag, coating it with a red powder, and then stabbed it into Mick's chest.

"Chiun, what the hell?" Stone asked as he saw the long stick jutting out from Mick's chest.

Chiun ignored him and, with a spinning movement that caused the ribbons attached to his robe to swirl around him like a silk tornado, slapped Mick's chest, embedding the stick into his heart.

Mick opened his eyes, drawing in a deep breath as his heart was jolted back to life. For a moment, he wondered if he was dead, but the stench of fish reminded him where he was. Chiun pulled the stick from his chest and scattered some of the red powder over the opening. He clapped Mick on the chest and a tingling sensation raced through Mick's entire body. He felt lightheaded.

"What happened?" Mick asked softly.

"You fell victim to a rare family illness. When I first met the trainer, he told me that Sinanju blood ran through everyone in your village. I did not believe him until the day I first saw you."

"Freya's thirteenth birthday," Mick whispered. The buzzing that had rattled his limbs had quieted to a dull tingling. He made a fist with both hands. He could feel his fingers.

"You showed signs of weakness that I recognized."

"So...I'm not dying?" Mick asked.

"Of course, you are dying. Everyone dies."

"But I'm not gonna die from this disease? What's it called?"

"Goo-chwee," Chiun replied. "It affects one or two of my villagers every generation."

"Goo-chwee?'" Mick asked, confused. "That means 'bad breath.' You're saying that I am dying of bad breath?"

"Your breathing is bad. If you cannot breathe, you will die."

"Wait, you knew he had this disease years ago?" Stone asked. "Why didn't you do something then?"

"The heart would pump most of the medicine away so the treatment is only effective after the heart stops."

"So he had to die first?" Stone asked.

"Why must I keep repeating myself to you?"

"What now?" Mick asked, moving his arms. They felt heavy and slow. "Am I cured?"

"Of course not," Chiun said. "Place the rest of these items back into the cylinder. The trainer will have to treat you every three moons to prevent the buildup of poisons in your blood."

"By stabbing me in the heart?"

"The armpits should do from now on," Chiun suggested. "Unless you die again. Just tell him not to pierce the same location."

Mick shook his head. What surprised him was that the headache was gone. He only felt as though he had a head cold.

"Are we now ready to finish the presentation?" Hyunsil asked.

Chiun looked around. Even though he had performed a rare and exquisite Dragon Pirouette to deliver the slap to Mick's chest, no one had noticed. And the villagers were already staring at the feast tables.

"He ruined the moment," Chiun said, motioning to Mick. "Eat."

At the suggestion, the villagers rushed to the feasting area, pulling the thin sheets off the tables, revealing piles of meat and small pastries.

Stone took a whiff. The roast pork actually smelled good. He smiled and headed for the large plates at the end of the table, only to be stopped by a single fingernail.

"Ouch! What's wrong now?"

"At your home, you may gorge on hamburgers," Chiun said, "but here, as a Sinanju trainee, you will eat appropriately."

Stone grimaced as his eyes searched the tables for Sinanju kosher food. He grabbed a few scraps of fish and a small bowl of rice. He glanced at Chiun and mumbled.

"Great feast…Grandmaster," he said with a forced smile.

CHAPTER TWENTY-SEVEN

Ben and Freya stood inside the front door of the Wilkins Building. Ben stared out the window.

"The cleaning crew should be here any minute," Ben said.

"Who are they?" Freya asked. "Can you trust them?"

"A team of specialists who are designed to secure a location. Normally, they erase any evidence that would reveal our activities. Today, they'll take everything here to Langley."

Freya looked at Ben and wondered if he ever smiled.

"Do you like your job?" Freya asked.

"I like accomplishing things. I like making a difference. That being said, I normally spend my days working underground, so it's nice to get out every now and then. Though I would be happier if 'getting out' didn't involve attacks from killer androids."

"I wanted to work for you because it meant working with Stone," Freya mused. "Today, I had to decide if the job was worth it for the job's sake."

"And?"

"For the first time in my life, I was afraid," Freya admitted. "I was embarrassed that I would fail."

Ben turned toward Freya and his smile disappeared.

"When that thing had you cornered, I wondered what I was doing putting a seventeen-year-old in the field. Then you showed me. Most people would have run if they had been in your shoes. Don't get me wrong; you're still green and you should have ran, but from what I saw today, you're going to do just fine."

"Will you tell Stone that?"

"I'm telling him to let you run the next op," Ben said. "There's the van," he said, nodding at a vehicle heading up the street. "Let's go."

~

Helmut sat inside a car parked down the block, where he watched Ben on a monitor. Even though Cole appeared to be speaking to himself, Helmut knew he was speaking with Freya. It frustrated him that he could not see her.

Fortunately for Helmut, Freya had only targeted Smirnoff's head. The rest of the body, where the key processors were located, was still mostly intact.

Helmut dialed a phone number as a gray and blue van arrived. "I see your vehicle. Have you taken care of the original crew?" he asked.

"Yes, sir," came the reply.

"Good," said Helmut. "Get the body."

As the van pulled in front of the lab, the side door opened, and eight men hopped out. After a few minutes, two men exited the building, struggling to carry an oversized duffel bag. They opened the back of the van, setting down the bag containing Smirnoff's body.

Helmut's phone rang. "We've obtained the android," a voice stated.

"Good work," Helmut replied. "Can you assess any damage?"

"Hard to tell at this point." Helmut could hear computer keystrokes in the background. "It looks like someone got in a couple of lucky shots. Smirnoff's brain is intact, but the motherboard is cracked."

"What about her memory?"

"We won't know until she's back online. Right now, I'm only giving her enough power to run diagnostics."

Helmut grimaced. Cole and his Sinanju trainee had taken Smirnoff's head, believing her brain would be inside, but there was a reason her torso had the most plating.

"To be honest, sir, she wasn't ready for battle."

"And yet she did remarkably well," Helmut said. "Once she is back online, we will increase shielding to her core components."

A brief pause was followed by a hesitant question. "Did McCabe…or Zelensky…make it?" the voice asked.

Helmut snarled into the phone. "Those names are never to be spoken around Smirnoff again. As far as she knows, they never existed. Is that clear?"

"Yes, sir."

"Prepare Smirnoff for transport. I'll have my men load her onto the plane."

In low power mode, Smirnoff could not move, but she could still hear everything around her.

Smirnoff created a new file in her base directory and added Helmut's picture. She labeled him *MAXIMAL THREAT*.

CHAPTER TWENTY-EIGHT

The villagers were still feasting at dusk, filling the center of the Sinanju square with stories of fishing, farming and ale. Before darkness fell, Hyunsil wheeled Mick to the House of Many Woods. Mick shook his head in awe as he looked around.

"I've taught classes about this House for years," he said. "But now that I'm here, it's more than I could have ever imagined. Thank you."

"It is my honor," Hyunsil said. "Wait here. I would like to give you something."

She walked to the next room and returned with a wooden fountain pen. The symbol for Sinanju was carved into the barrel and edged in delicate filigree.

"I can't take that," Mick said.

"Each caretaker bestows a gift to their successor," Hyunsil said, bowing. "For the past several generations, the gifts have been fountain pens. They write better than the quills that Master Chiun prefers. My father died before he could give me one, but this is the one I made for my successor."

"You carved this?" Mick asked, looking at the intricate work.

"Besides caring for the House and teaching the children, I have a lot of spare time. Do not worry, I will make another."

"I don't know what to say…wait a second," Mick said and then reached into his pocket. He handed her a small object wrapped in red silk. "I've been trying to give this to you, but I was too busy dying."

Hyunsil unwrapped the cloth to reveal an opal pendant. It was engraved in gold with the symbol for the House of Sinanju.

"Kojong ordered this to be returned to the village if we were ever reunited," Mick said. "I'm giving this to you in hope of that day. I never dreamed I would be the one returning it."

"I recognize this pendant, but I do not understand," Hyunsil said. "Kojing reported that this opal as well as a large lavaliere necklace had been stolen during one of his absences. There have been many questions about this over the years."

"I think I can help fill in the blanks," Mick said, smiling. "Kojing gave the opal to Kojong as a memento. The necklace was provided in case he needed a dowry, which was common in many of the eastern nations. He did. The necklace is buried with Kojong's first wife."

Hyunsil smiled.

"Thank you for your lesson, Caretaker," she said and leaned over to give him a hug.

Mick blushed.

"Least I could do."

"Do you have any other questions while you are here?" Hyunsil asked.

"Too many to ask in one lifetime," Mick said. "But one comes to mind. Kojong made a pretty extensive copy of the records for us, detailing Masters of Sinanju until his time."

"What would you like to know?"

"What is the one thing you wished that someone had told you when you took over the records?"

Hyunsil looked around the room in thought and then she grinned.

"Always be somewhat …skeptical of the Masters' stories."

"I was taught to treat our records like gospel," Mick said. "We were taught to write down as much detail as possible."

"This is our standard as well, but while the Masters of Sinanju are amazing, do not forget that they are still human."

"Wait, you mean some of those things are embellished?" Mick asked and then laughed out loud. "Our Sunny Joes have been feeling like they are missing some core part of the training because the Korean Masters are described as being so powerful!"

"Let us just say that the victor gets to write history, and the House of Sinanju is forever the victor."

"Of course we are," a thin, reedy voice chimed from behind. Chiun glided into the room wearing a subdued black kimono.

"How long are we staying?" Mick asked.

"Young Kim shall send a whirlbird for us in three days."

"Good. That gives me some time to catch up," Mick said. "By the way, Hyunsil said that you wanted me to stay in the wheelchair? I feel good enough to walk."

"If it appeared that I instantly healed you, there would be no end to the requests," Chiun whispered. "I would be pestered to cure everything from hair loss to foot boils."

"Mick, it will be my honor to pilot your chair," Hyunsil said, bowing low, but careful not to bow lower than she did for Chiun.

"This has been the trip of a lifetime," Mick said. "Sometime, if it's possible, you'll have to visit the reservation. It's nowhere near as beautiful as this, but it's much warmer."

"That would be wonderful. Shall we continue our tour?"

"Oh yeah! I've only read about this stuff," Mick said, looking around until his eyes settled on a large patch of what looked to be iron scales hanging on the wall. "To be honest, when I read 'dragon scale mat' I thought they were talking about a lizard."

"What is the confusion? A dragon is a dragon and a lizard is a lizard," Chiun explained.

Mick wheeled himself to the front trophy room and Hyunsil turned toward Chiun. "If it does not offend the Master, might I use the telephone to keep in touch with our tribal brothers from time to time?"

Chiun considered the request and then nodded.

"Only if you call collect."

CHAPTER TWENTY-NINE

The sun had set, and the feast was winding down. Stone returned to his hut and sat on the floor. He could not imagine how difficult it would be to live here, with the pervasive stink and bitter cold.

Stone took a deep breath to center himself. His lungs had healed enough that the pain was manageable. He realized, with some surprise, that he did not crave a cigarette. He could not even remember the last time he had gone more than two days without one.

As Stone gazed out the small window, he saw that the moon cast two huge shadows from the Horns, which spread over the village. During the day, the Horns were powerful and majestic monuments, but in moonlight, they looked eerie.

If he was going to check the top of the Horn, it would have to be now. He did not know when he would be in the village next — if ever — and even the thought of Chiun cleansing his kidneys would not keep him from trying. He had to know what was up there.

Stone slipped on his jacket and slowly opened the door. A breeze reminded him just how cold it was outside.

He moved silently through the village. As soon as he made it to the Horn, he began climbing. He stopped halfway up, expecting to see a bright red kimono headed his way like a thunderbolt, but there was no movement other than a few of the villagers who had remained to clean up after the feast. Was it really going to be this easy?

Stone finally reached the top. It was just as jagged as he had seen in his dream. For a moment, he hesitated to crawl to the other side of the Horn. *How much of his dream would turn out to be true?*, he wondered.

Taking one last glance back at the village, satisfied that even Chiun could not stop him at this point, Stone scuttled around the Horn and found the small carved-out nook from his dream. The air seemed to get colder as he leaned toward the hole.

He did not find a skull inside, but something was reflecting light from the back.

Stone reached in with his hand. He pulled out the new package of cigarettes Chiun had taken on the flight over.

"Blast it, Chiun, I thought you flushed these!" Stone said, placing them in his pocket.

Was Chiun somehow able to make him dream about this? How else would he know about the small opening or the jagged top? Or was he half-remembering something Sunny Joe had said about them? Stone made his way back down the Horn and walked along the muddy path to the village. He entered his hut and slammed the door, not caring who heard him. He pulled the cigarettes from his pocket and stared at them.

He knew that he was going to hear a lecture when Chiun saw him. *Was this his chance to stop smoking?*, he wondered to himself. Even if he chose not to continue with his Sinanju training, it made sense. His skills would deteriorate much more quickly if he continued to smoke.

And there, in the solitude of a cold wooden hut, with the final decision weighing on his shoulders, Stone sighed and opened the pack.

Just one more, he thought and pulled out his lighter. *We aren't leaving for a few days.*

"He has squandered my gift," Chiun said as he saw a small light flicker from Stone's hut. "The boy refuses to embrace the strength of his Korean heart."

"Should you not have told him the truth about his dream?" Hyunsil asked, glancing at the skull Chiun had removed from the top of the Horn.

"After we leave, you will call the Trainer to inform him that the boy has been called to The Trials."

"He is too young and inexperienced to fight in the Master's Trial."

"The Trial has come early at times in the past," Chiun said. "Sinanju has survived."

"Could his father not battle in his stead?" Hyunsil asked and then lowered her head. "It has been done before."

Chiun's hazel eyes narrowed.

"An embarrassing fluke like that will *never* happen again," he replied bitterly. "The son of Remo Williams will answer the call, or he will die."

EPILOGUE

It had been almost a week since Eleanora had traveled to Nornswain. The newly-crowned Queen Mother of the Lakluun people had made the trip to the small island hidden in the North Atlantic against the advice of her new council. They told her that it was not yet time for the Master's Trial. They pointed out that since she was now Queen Mother, the Lakluun had no champion.

Eleanora would not listen to their entreaties. She sent a messenger to Russia, while she left for Nornswain.

The island was tiny. Its sole edifice was an arena, constructed from slabs of Norse marble during the time when Babylon still ruled much of the world. Large decorated columns were set at eight-foot intervals surrounding the arena.

After she arrived, Eleanora lit the brazier at the center of the arena, poking and prodding until the fire grew large enough to maintain itself. As Queen Mother, she would never be expected to manually light a fire herself, but on Nornswain, she was merely one of The Six. Eleanora tended the fire until the flames reached a large amethyst globe perched at the center of the stone fixture.

As the globe began to glow, Eleanora breathed in deeply and smiled. She enjoyed listening to the salty splash of the Atlantic Ocean. It reminded her of home — at least, the way her home had been before her people were betrayed by the Sinanju.

Eleanora grabbed two stones, resting on an iron ring circling below the amethyst globe. She engraved a name on the back of each of the stones and returned them to the ring.

Now all she could do was wait.

Before she was Queen Mother, Eleanora had been the Lakluun Champion. Had everything gone as it should have, she would have been the one to fight in the Master's Trial for Lakluun honor. But the Sinanju girl had ruined everything.

~

The Master's Trial had always been an imperfect compromise. Shortly after the dawn of man, twelve unique tribes emerged. Eventually, the tribes grew in size and power until they began crossing into other tribes' boundaries. The result was war, culminating in the decimation of six of the original tribes. The leaders of the remaining tribes declared a truce, desperate to keep their people alive.

The terms of their treaty stated that once every generation, each tribal leader would gather on Nornswain Island to start the ceremony they had come to call "The Masters' Trial."

Nornswain had been chosen because of its neutral location and inhospitable nature.

After arriving, the leaders would greet each other in peace and engrave the name of their greatest champion onto a stone and place it on the iron ring above the pit. After the fire scorched the champion's name into the stone, the amethyst globe would signal each Champion of their selection.

Each Champion would then meet for a battle to the death. The winner would ensure free passage of their people throughout all parts of the world for the next generation. The remaining tribes would restrict their activities to their own borders.

~

Three days after lighting the brazier, Eleanora was awakened by a horn. The haunting moan of air twisted through carved channels of bone. She notched an arrow and silently moved behind one of the rocks at the island's edge.

Though not yet dawn, the moon provided enough light for Eleanora to pick out the image of an approaching vessel.

As it neared, she could tell that it was an ancient hand-carved boat, carrying a man old enough to have built it himself.

Eleanora returned the arrow to her quiver and waited for the stranger in the center of the arena. The brazier was still burning when the man entered. His skin was marble-white, and he wore brightly-beaded armor trimmed with dark fur. His graying hair was tied into a knot, allowing it to flow through the back of a tall golden crown. Though his frame was imposing, it was obvious that he was past his prime.

"Peace!" the man said with a hearty smile. "I am Vitomir, King of Magog. I have traveled from the Kara Sea to answer the Lakluun."

"Peace! I am Eleanora, Queen Mother of the Lakluun people."

Vitomir looked confused for a moment and then his eyes narrowed. His village had been banned from the last Master's Trial as punishment for initiating an early attack. But Vitomir was familiar with the other tribes, especially the Lakluun. Before the Trials, their two tribes were personal enemies. He was familiar with their Monarch/Mage system.

"Are you Queen or Mother?" Vitomir asked.

"I am both," Eleanora said.

"Lakluun has always had a King."

"My King is dead," Eleanora said. "I rule in his stead."

"I heard of the attack. He had no sons?"

"I am the only surviving member of the Lakluun rulers. I am here to claim our place in the Trials."

Vitomir hesitated. Something was wrong.

"The brazier has been lit," Eleanora said, motioning to the fire. "Your stone is ready."

"The call is too early," Vitomir protested. "Our champion is not yet ready."

"When are any of us *really* ready?" Eleanora asked. "We have sent generations of our best warriors to be slaughtered by the Sinanju, and for what?"

"The Trials have reinforced peace among our villages for centuries," Vitomir said. "You know this. The time before the Masters' Trial was filled with chaos and death — we were nearly driven to extinction!"

"Were we?" Eleanora asked. "Or are we just been believing whatever the Sinanju tell us?"

"If this is about taking vengeance upon the Sinanju, it will not end well for you."

"I have prepared for the Sinanju in ways that will change the Trials forever," Eleanora said, motioning to the fire.

Vitomir reached toward the iron ring and pulled out two darkened rocks. One carried the doubled ellipsis of the Lakluun.

The other was emblazoned with the slashed trapezoid of the Sinanju.

"The Sinanju have already been here?" he asked.

Eleanora said nothing.

"Who struck the name 'Winston' on their stone?"

"It is not your concern. Their champion has been named."

Vitomir flipped the Lakluun stone over.

"Who is Freya of Lakluun?" he asked.

"She is the reason that the Sinanju will finally lose," Eleanora gloated. "She is trained in Sinanju, but Lakluun by blood. She will fight for us."

Vitomir smiled and then began to laugh.

"This is your plan?" Vitomir asked. "You have blinded yourself with hatred."

"Perhaps, but you still have a choice to make," Eleanora said, handing him a stone. "The call has gone out. You must engrave the name of your champion, or forfeit your place in the Trials."

Vitomir looked at the stone in his hand, then back at Eleanora.

"Magog will not submit to your demands," he said. "Do what you will. We will send the champion of our choice."

"No one will recognize your champion if his name is not engraved on this stone."

Vitomir stepped toward Eleanora but this time, she saw pity in his eyes.

"Do you not see what is happening? You are burning with vengeance and willing to destroy all of us in the process."

"I *will* have revenge," Eleanora admitted. "But it will be within the rules."

"Such as choosing the champion for the Sinanju?" he asked.

"They have cheated us long enough," Eleanora said. "Stand with me."

Vitomir spit on the ground before Eleanora.

"Magog will have no part of your madness."

He lifted his stone in front of Eleanora and broke it in half.

"My people are free," he said and walked off.

"You have forever banished your people to their village!" Eleanora shouted out after him.

Vitomir turned and charged toward Eleanora. "Child, you have taken this too far! If this were not neutral ground, I would..."

Eleanora pulled her sword so quickly that Vitomir did not see it enter his ribcage. She twisted the sword hard enough to snap the blade inside his chest.

"You would do nothing!" Eleanora shouted into his dying face. "The call to challenge has gone forth! The Master's Trial will mark the death of Sinanju!"

THE END

ALSO AVAILABLE:

FORGOTTEN SON

Will Stone and Freya, the lethal brother-sister duo, be enough to help their new boss Benjamin Cole stop the Great Mexican Ninja Army from invading the southwestern United States?

Also available as an audiobook!

THE KILLING FIELDS

Her name is 14. All she really wants is a new best friend...but it's hard to make friends with someone you're trying to kill. Stone and Freya must face off against a bionic killer while inside a nuclear death trap!

OVERLOAD

A figure from Sunny Joe's past seeks revenge by hiring Stone and Freya for a video game where there are no cheat codes...and death is for real!

If you like Jerry's work on Legacy, then you'll love the action and satire of *The Last Witness*!

www.TheLastWitness.com

GERALD WELCH

JERRY WELCH is a double-edged threat, both writer and graphic artist. The self-described literary bastard of Warren Murphy and Richard Sapir, Jerry is best known for the writing and artwork in his "Last Witness" series. **www.TheLastWitness.com**

Jerry prefers to be known as one of only four people on Earth ever to be granted the title "Honorary Master of Sinanju."

His personal website is **www.JerryWelch.com**, where he's always blogging about something or other.

WARREN MURPHY

WARREN MURPHY was born in Jersey City, where he worked in journalism and politics until launching the Destroyer series with Richard Sapir in 1971. A screenwriter (*Lethal Weapon II*, *The Eiger Sanction*) as well as a novelist, Murphy's work has won more than a dozen national awards, including multiple Edgars and Shamuses.

A Korean War veteran, Murphy served on the board of the Mystery Writers of America, and has been a member of the Screenwriters Guild, the Private Eye Writers of America, the International Association of Crime Writers, and the American Crime Writers League. He has five children: Deirdre, Megan, Brian, Ardath, and Devin.

"I AM CREATED SHIVA, THE DESTROYER; DEATH, THE SHATTERER OF WORLDS. THE DEAD NIGHT TIGER MADE WHOLE BY THE MASTER OF SINANJU. WHO IS THIS DOG MEAT THAT DARES CHALLENGE ME?"

Made in United States
Orlando, FL
08 June 2025

61936006R00133